SEASON V

SEASON V

A NOVEL

for Cathy

Randy L Allen

6-10-17

RANDY ALLEN

LIBRARY OF CONGRESS CONTROL NUMBER: 2015914335
ISBN: HARDCOVER   978-1-5144-0357-0
             SOFTCOVER   978-1-5144-0353-2
             EBOOK   978-1-5144-0352-5

Printed in the United States of America by BookMasters, Inc
Ashland OH
October 2015

Rev. date: 09/02/2015

To order additional copies of this book, contact:
Xlibris
1-888-795-4274
www.Xlibris.com
Orders@Xlibris.com
719517

CONTENTS

The Preseason

Week 1

Lt. Gen. Dave Duncan looked around the small private conference room attached to his suite of offices at Ft. Monroe, Virginia. He reflected back to his days as a second lieutenant, when to have been summoned to this office would have been the most nerve-wracking thing he could imagine. Now this was his empire. As the commanding general of the Training and Doctrine Command (TRADOC), he was now responsible for the training of the force. At least he reminded himself for the part of training that took place in a schoolhouse setting.

Around the conference table were three of the best US Army Rangers he had ever encountered. There was Lt. Col. Barry Bogues, Lt. Col. Samuel Cauble, and Maj. William Stidham. They had been assembled by him to hear of a new proposal being presented to the joint chiefs of staff. The army rangers had been resurrected during the conflict in Vietnam after having disappeared after World War II and Korea. Their training had been conducted on the ground in country by men who were trying to practice the survival arts while teaching young men at the same time. His proposed idea for the JCS might just give them an edge on getting this arduous mission accomplished.

He had floated and gotten approval on a trial basis to establish a training regimen for this skill set in CONUS (Continental United States). These men were about to hear a bodacious plan to implement his idea.

"Good morning," he began to speak, and all eyes were quickly on him. "I hope you are all well. There is a matter of great importance that I need your help implementing. This matter concerns the training of our young rangers, who will soon be coming to take our places. You three men know firsthand how vital a role these men will have in the future as we defend our country." He paused and looked around the room. The thought flashed through his brain, *Good, I've got them now.*

Quickly, he moved on to his first point, "Men, I think you all know one another, but for the benefit of my staff, let me introduce you." He went around the table. He detailed the career highlights of each of these warriors, the schools

1

they had attended, the honors they had accumulated, and the number of tours they had done in Vietnam. Then he caught some by surprise when he asked them, "During your tours in Vietnam, roughly how many rangers were you responsible for training?"

There was no response at first, so he looked to Lieutenant Colonel Bogues. "Just a rough estimate will do." Bogues and the other two had all done three tours in-country. Calculating hurriedly in his mind, he came up with a rough guess of thirty-five.

Moving on to Lt. Col. Cauble, who was similarly unprepared for the question, he received his answer, "Well, sir, using the SWAG (Scientific Wild-Ass Guess) method of estimating, I calculate about forty." His answer was short and to the point. He had no idea of the real number, nor did it matter.

Looking over to Stidham, the general grinned and said, "And I'll bet you would guess about forty-five, Bill."

Stidham smiled and said, "I was actually thinking about forty-three, sir." Everyone in the room sensed the general's mood and laughed heartily at his humor.

"As you can see, the point is not how many you have trained, but how well they were trained under your guidance. Folks, I will tell you now, these three men have consistently been the leaders of our force in the field, not from a command point of view, but from the perspective of developing the doctrine of how best to use the rangers in the total force package. That is why I am challenging you three to develop the curriculum and course standards for our new ranger school. You will each develop your prototype school and an exhaustive final training evaluation for your students. Then we will look at the three products, and we may adopt one, but more likely we will take elements from all the prototypes and adapt the methodology to our final product."

"Gentlemen, I don't have to tell you how important this mission is. This is a unique and exclusive opportunity to leave your footprint on the history of the rangers. The products you develop will be the basis of our training program for years to come. My staff will support you. We have established budget accounts and funding requirements for each installation you will be operating upon these for the duration. Are there any questions?"

Bogues was first. "Sir, where will the schools be housed? Will they all be at the same location?"

The general answered, "You will be at Bragg, Cauble will be at Benning, and Stidham at Campbell. I have had several individuals come to me with scenarios they find palatable for the final exercise. I will be putting some of them in touch with you for your consideration. Be aware that none of these are mandatory. You have the leeway to develop your own more meaningful scenario or adapt their proposals into other formats."

Three days later, Stidham had arrived at Ft. Campbell. He had completed his in-processing and been given temporary office space in the headquarters. He was becoming comfortable with the environment in which he would be working. He had finished his morning workout when he had heard the knock on his door.

Marty Bringle hurried from his guest quarters room on Ft. Campbell. The agency plane would be arriving at Campbell Army Airfield in thirty minutes. He wanted to be there to catch it when it came in. He had to hurry to get there. He was headed for Washington. His new job in the headquarters had been a study in problems. Having spent twenty-nine years in the service of the government, he was accustomed to dealing with problems. This was a new type of problem he had had to learn about. It was no longer about managing field assets, which he had proven more than capable of doing. But the agency had brought him to the main office with a nice boost in his pay to give him a couple of years to pad his retirement pension he would soon qualify to draw. No one had told him this, so he continued to try to make a name for himself by involving himself in any project he saw come along. This had led to his trip to Ft. Campbell to meet with Maj. William Stidham.

After his initial reluctance to involve himself in agency affairs, Stidham had seemed to be impressed with the accomplishments Bringle had been able to bring to Stidham's new project. Bringle knew that much work remained to be done to bring this project into the fold, so that his "hare-brained scheme" could be developed into an actual plan with the hope of being performed as a mission. Stidham had labeled it upon hearing the rough draft of it and he didn't seem interested in changing his mind.

Bringle had just learned that the Austrian nationalized citizen, currently serving as secretary of state, had scheduled another round of peace talks in Paris. If he had no interruptions, he planned to be on that government-owned Boeing 727 headed for Paris that evening. He had been officially detailed as part of the negotiating team as a minor functionary in the agricultural attaché's delegation for these talks. He suspected upon his first trip to Paris that the French and the North Vietnamese both were aware that he didn't know a lot about any agriculture and particularly not about what passed for agriculture in South Vietnam. He really didn't care what they thought as long as he continued to get a seat at the table.

During the delegation's first trip to Paris, not much excitement had happened at the negotiations. But one evening, while at dinner at one of the many elegant French restaurants, he had been startled to see Cho Dinh in the restaurant. He vaguely recognized Cho as one of the industrial experts on the North Vietnamese delegation. He realized that Cho was walking toward him. As Bringle had studied what to do, Dinh had noticed something on the floor, leaned over and picked it up, handed it to a passing waiter, and turned on his heel and was gone. Only after realizing whom he had just been approached by did Bringle notice the scrap of paper lying on his table.

He thought, *This guy is pretty good to have put this over on me.* Unhurriedly, he palmed the paper, got up, and headed to the restaurant's lavatory. Entering a stall in the room, only then did he look at the paper. There were eight numbers on the paper and the words "for 100,000 the schedule" This had made no sense to him.

As for the message, Bringle had no idea as to what it referred. As he sat at the table, finishing his meal, it dawned on him that he had to make a phone call. Finishing his red wine, he left what he considered a generous tip, paid his bill, and hurried back to the hotel where the delegation was being housed. He grabbed a folder and went to the operations suite, where secure lines had been installed. He figured the time difference back to Washington and realized it was three o'clock in the afternoon there. He probably could reach the assistant director of operations at the agency.

Timothy Barstow was in his office. He heard the phone ring and picked it up. There was Bringle. Barstow was only slightly annoyed; he had dealt with the man for years and had learned to tolerate him if not to like him. Truth be known, it had been his idea to get Bringle into the home office to finish his career. Some days he regretted the decision. The man could not sit still and let the meter run until it was time to go home for the final time.

Barstow spoke into the handheld receiver. "Yes, Bringle, what can I do for you?" Bringle quickly recounted the evening's events. After listening to his reconstituted account, Barstow knew no more than Bringle, but the latter felt much better that he had reported the suspicious action and therefore was covered by the agency.

After some discussion, Barstow decided, "You continue with your work at the mission. Maybe there will be some further contact. Have that note with you at all times but not in the open. Watch this man, but make no overt advances to him. He probably is being watched. If there is anything further to come, he will make the advance.

Bringle had not liked the idea but had no better solution in mind. He proceeded with the plan. He had been courteous to Dinh during sessions in which both were involved but had not spoken directly to him. There had been no further contact or, for that matter, even the hint that there was any recognition. Bringle began to wonder if he had misread the actions of that evening.

Two days later, the peace talk mission had come to a temporary halt, and the delegation had returned to Washington. When Marty Bringle reported to work the next day, he was flabbergasted to find that the ADO had left him a message. Bringle had been included in the team to represent the agency. Since these talks did not seem likely to bear fruit any time soon, the agency had tabbed Bringle to represent them while posing as low-level Department of Agriculture member. It seemed that ADO Barstow wanted to see him ASAP. With some trepidation, Bringle took the elevator to the seventh floor.

Walking into the office of the ADO, he was waved directly into the office. Barstow greeted him warmly. Bringle was surprised by this as he was generally not highly regarded within the walls of his agency. Bringle was beginning to realize that something big was going to happen. Barstow grabbed the phone, waited a moment, and then said, "He's here. Can you join us."

Barstow explained that they would be joined by Pete Carter, senior analyst for the agency on all matters Vietnamese. Bringle and Carter had been acquainted for many years; their relationship had always been just that—acquainted.

Barstow explained, "I asked Pete to look at your message, and by the way, do you have it? Pete has come up with an interesting theory. Pete, why don't you fill in the details?" Barstow was already examining the scrap of paper that was becoming dog-eared from being carried in Bringle's pocket. He was glad to be rid of it.

Meanwhile, Carter intoned, "When I got this, I couldn't make heads or tails of it. After a few hours, I thought I recognized something in the digits. I asked one of our interns to check it out. She confirmed my suspicions. This set of digits corresponds to a set of grid coordinates on the topographical map of North Vietnam used by our pilots when they are paying their little visits to that neighborhood." Reaching into a manila file folder he had brought with him, he pushed several photos of a small group of nondescript huts toward Bringle. "This is what is located at those coordinates." He went on to explain that analysis had suggested nothing noteworthy of the area. Playing a hunch, he had asked for a week of staggered U-2 flights with camera reports to him daily. On the third day, there had appeared a few North Vietnam Army (NVA) personnel moving about the area. He produced the day 3 photos. Again, nothing happened for a few days. Then this morning, we found this. Again, a new set of photos. These were the photos Bringle had shown Stidham later in his effort to get the cooperation of the army ranger.

Bringle had been impressed. "Those U-2 fellows do a heck of a job for a group that doesn't exist." He chuckled at his own joke. They all considered the irony of this. The U-2 program had never been acknowledged by the government even though one of the planes had been shot down and the pilot captured during a flight over Soviet airspace several years earlier.

Quickly, Barstow brought the group back to the reality of the moment. "I would like you to continue your contacts with Mr. Dinh at any further negotiations that may be held. If he attempts to contact you through other channels, make yourself available to him." Turning to Carter, he continued, "Pete, please request an extension of the U-2 flights."

"How long do we do the flyovers?" queried Carter.

"Let's set it for a week from today" was the answer from Barstow.

Bringle had started requesting topographic maps of the area. He had learned the proximity to the coast and to the Ho Chi Minh Trail, as it was known. This incursion path into the South was really not a trail but a fairly large area as wide as fifty miles in places and including territory supposedly controlled by Laos and Cambodia. Owing to the large number of NVA and advisory troops from allies of the Hanoi regime, it was well-known that the area was not under the control of anyone except the person who stood on it that day. He might not control that segment the next day. This area had been bombed repeatedly by the USAF with napalm and Agent Orange and when likely targets could be identified with traditional warheads as available. Despite all these efforts, the area remained subject to infiltration by NVA forces.

On the third subsequent day, the flyover had resulted in photos, which, after analysis, appeared to show the arrival of three American POWs into the compound. The group had remained there for four days, and then they disappeared. The excitement level in Foggy Bottom was growing exponentially. Barstow said to Carter and Bringle during their daily briefing on the flight results, "We may be able to get some of these guys out." Bringle, whose field experience had bred some caution into him, replied, "I do wonder what he meant by a schedule for the site! If we knew that, we could really make hay."

Maj. William Stidham looked across the desk of the small office he had recently inherited from someone unknown to him. He gazed in amazement at the man sitting there who had just proposed the most audacious undertaking he could imagine. This man, who Stidham had known for twelve years, had always been a loose cannon, even in the murky world of agency-infested operations in Southeast Asia. Stidham was wondering quite frankly if Marty Bringle had finally flipped completely over the edge.

"You want me to what?" he once again asked the operative.

"Let me explain it like this," replied Bringle who had spent a decade in the backwater areas of places such as Cambodia, Laos, and even into regions of North Vietnam. "You haven't seen me around operations for the past year and a half because I have been moved to HQs. Not that I thought you or anyone else out there would miss me. I assure you that there are talks going on between the Austrian and the North to give them all that God-forsaken country so we can cut our losses and get the hell out."

Stidham looked at him calmly and stated, "I understood that part, but I don't see what that has to do with me. I've done my three tours over there, and I was just getting settled here in developing the prototype for the new ranger school. After eighteen years, they finally asked me for some input into what is being brought into the ranger skill set."

"Well, you see, I have it on good authority that there is a POW transfer point in North Vietnam that we can hit and rescue some guys who are about to become guests in the Hanoi Hilton. Of course, if you have no interest . . ." Bringle allowed his voice to trail away as he watched Stidham for his response. Stidham eyed the manila envelope on the desk between them. He wondered what it contained.

"Is this your good authority in this package?" he queried the agency man. "Care to play show and tell?"

Bringle nonchalantly nudged the envelope toward Stidham. Stidham picked up the envelope and saw it contained several photos. As he eyed them, he wondered aloud, "Taken by agency assets on the ground?"

Bringle shook his head. "Taken by U-2 this morning of a little village called Dong Ha. It sits just nineteen miles from Hanoi. We've identified four positively as downed AF personnel. We believe there may be two more MC personnel and possibly a third unknown POW being held in this cozy little contraption."

Nodding, Stidham examined the background more closely. "Have you analyzed historical footage of other flyovers to establish the history of this place, or did it just pop up?" As he said this, a dozen follow-up questions exploded in his brain, things such as authenticity, timing, reliability of source, the motivation of that source, the location of the source, consequences to the source if exposed, and perhaps, most importantly, what would it take to retrieve what the agency referred to as assets; but in his vernacular, they were just people.

With a noticeable shift in enthusiasm, he asked, "Has this been cleared through the top?"

His meaning was "had the joint chiefs of staff or even the army chief of staff been briefed on the existence of the evidence he had just seen?" Knowing the source, he felt a need to know if he was being recruited for an approved operation or if this was going to be a black operation. He thought of Bringle's reputation and knew the answer to the question. If he showed any desire to go further with this, he was about to depart from the DOD Vietnam War and become part of the clandestine CIA secret war that he had heard of through backroom whispers and off the record talks with other officers and had brushed elbows with its practitioners from time to time.

He knew that his record of service first as an airborne infantry officer and then as a long-range patrol, followed by a stint as a long-range reconnaissance patrol, followed by the army's decision to revitalize the World War II branch known as the rangers was not unknown, not only to this man, but also to others throughout the underground, non-reported war participants whose informal network was extensive through the entire region known as SEATO or the Southeast Asian Treaty Organization.

He also knew that if he could be convinced of the authenticity of the evidence he held, he would never be able to walk away from the chance to bring back any

American serviceman who was being held in the hellhole little cages he could see in the background of at least three of the photos he had just examined.

Bringle looked at him and said, "What do I need to do to convince you?" He knew he had won the skirmish to get his man, but he also must seal the deal with him.

Stidham looked at him steadily and spoke slowly. "I want independent corroboration, both of the photos and of the analysis from AF and MI, not agency resources."

Bringle grinned as he reached into his briefcase and slid the TWIX receipts for both items to Stidham. "Will these serve your purposes, or do I need to provide the detailed report from MI? There is also preliminary analysis of photo-imagery confirming the identity of three pilots in the photos. I believe you have to think my source is pretty good."

"But what makes you think they will be there when we put together a team, rehearse the mission, and deploy to theatre?" Stidham's objection was out in a flash, but once again, Bringle had an answer.

"My source tells me that this is a way station used for the temporary holding of prisoners on the way to Hanoi. Granted these guys may not be there by the time we get our team into position. But I do have every confidence that there will be more guys coming through the confines, so to speak. Bringle sounded almost smug when talking about his source, Stidham noted, but he also could feel his cushy assignment in the states slipping away from him in a very rapid manner. He was beginning to realize that he had been persuaded to undertake one last mission to Vietnam; his last feeble arguments were soon turned into agreements by Bringle's persuasive abilities.

Stidham finally rationalized in his mind the fact that he was going to say yes, but he decided to buy a little time to mull over what he knew would be the answer. "How much time do I have to decide?" He offered this lamely and knew that he had decided already.

Bringle responded with a wave, "Take as long as you need. I don't anticipate making this offer to any of your colleagues before tomorrow. Shall we say we will meet here again tomorrow, at let's say 0900."

Stidham stood up to leave, knowing he would be there, with a growing unease about how the CIA man had just taken over his personal office space in the headquarters of Ft. Campbell, Kentucky.

That evening, in his quarters, he began to make some calls to some of the senior NCOs and junior officers he had planned to invite to become part of the temporary cadre of the version of the ranger school he had long envisioned and was now at the crossroads of establishing. He had a need to contact these men that had just become ever more pressing than the founding of his beloved ranger school. As he explained his ideas to these men, he began to extend offers of assignments to those whom he had come to trust through their mutual experiences shared as brothers in arms during his three tours of duty in Vietnam. Before turning in for the night, he had contacted eight men who considered it an honor to be asked by their mentor to join his team. He chuckled to himself. Well, at least no one had yet turned him down.

The next day, at 0700, he stood in the office of Ms. Vickie Cross, who had worked in the headquarters of the 101st Division (Air Assault) as it had become known during its current deployment to the Republic of Vietnam for at least twenty-five years since the unit had come marching home from World War II, then known as the 101st Infantry Division (Airborne). They had been her Screaming Eagles ever since. Her present position was that of military personnel officer or MILPO as the army termed them.

She looked at the new major who had reported in to the HQ Company just a few days before. She liked his looks. Not only was he handsome in a down-home sort of way, but he also came in showing her the courtesy that many of the field grade officers, rampant in a division headquarters, seemed to have trouble mastering. Not only that, but it was also obvious that the major had already done his morning physical training (PT) routine and had also taken care of his personal hygiene. Additionally, he stood before her in clean, freshly starched fatigues that had obviously been tailored to maximize the impressive appearance he wished to present. She decided that if he had half a mind, he would become one of her boys. She was a mother to those who needed it—a grandmother to some—but she dearly loved the boys of the 101st.

She suddenly realized that she was looking at the new face of her beloved unit. The men who had gone to Vietnam from Ft. Campbell so many years ago would not be returning there when the division redeployed in the near future. She would know almost none of them. But she resolved that in the days to come, they would become her boys just as those who had gone from her had.

Stidham shifted his weight uneasily and decided to break the silence of the office. "Ms. Cross, they tell me that you are the MILPO here, and all personnel transactions begin with you", he stammered slightly as he introduced the idea of his visit to her. "Well, ma'am, I have been tasked with establishing an army ranger prototype course here, which may become the schematic for the future of the rangers. For me to do this, I will need the assistance of a team."

"Yes, Major Stidham, I am aware of your tasking here. If you would prepare the forms requesting personnel, I would be happy to requisition those personnel needed to fill those slots." She turned to search her files for the required forms needed to modify the table of organization and equipment. She was startled when she turned back to the major to hand him the forms when she realized he was holding a small stack of personnel requisition forms in his hand and extending them to her.

"I have taken the liberty of filling these out for the soldiers I will require. They have all indicated their willingness to accept the assignment even though some of them have not been at their current slots long enough to rotate under normal circumstances. I do believe that the case for immediacy can be made due to the urgency of the tasking." Stidham smiled with his boyish charm as he placed the requisitions on her desk blotter.

Vickie Cross was not accustomed to officers who could complete their own paperwork, and she was suspicious of those who tried, often finding them utterly incompetent in this world of hers. She began to leaf through the pages, which seemed to be well-prepared at first blush, but she knew full well that she would have to go through them with her fine tooth comb to get them corrected and in order.

Stidham was speaking again before she looked up. "Ma'am, I meant no disrespect but was merely trying to enhance our working arrangement going forward. But I will require these soldiers to be here ASAP. Is there anything else I can do to expedite this process?"

"Major, I appreciate your efforts, but I will need to look at these closely before submitting them to DA (Department of the Army). Normally, there will be a wait of at least three months to enact such a transaction. If some of these require waivers from losing commands due to mission expediencies, this time may be even longer." She smiled sweetly at the major and thought this will cook his goat. He had the most disarming demeanor as he received this bad news, so she thought to add a little salt to his wound and added, "Welcome to the world of headquarters, where nothing happens immediately."

Stidham simply nodded and said, "Thank you for your time. I do hope you have a nice day." He then turned on his heel and left the office. He was thinking that his plans for the ranger school were probably doomed by the inertia inherent in so many military organizations. He felt that he had just discovered again why he liked leading soldiers in the field instead of commanding them from behind a desk. He moved with a purpose toward the office he had been assigned in the mammoth headquarters building and thought of his 0900 meeting with Bringle. He suddenly brightened when he realized that the other two guys who were in the development phase were likely getting the same treatment as he was.

As he walked into the office, he saw the back of a visitor's head and realized that he would not have to wait until 0900 for the meeting to transpire with Bringle. Seated in the chair on the visitor's side of the desk was the man he had last seen several years ago in South Vietnam. His mind was operating furiously as he fought to make sense of the situation he found himself entangled.

He had been given a tasking that he dearly wanted to complete before his military career was over. However, it looked like the support he would need to affect the program he envisioned was sorely lacking as he proceeded. On top of this, he was now faced with Bringle and his harebrained scheme to pull off the rescue of some number of American PWs from the jungles of another continent. Given the lack of success he had just encountered in trying to obtain personnel and the discouraging news about their possible reassignments to his team, he felt like Bringle needed to find another guinea pig for his project. He was thoroughly disgusted, but he remembered the creed of the ranger, "Lead the way." Having thus reminded himself of his commitment, he looked at Bringle one last time from the rear and felt the beginning of an inspiration in his mind.

"Good morning, William," began Bringle when he became aware of the presence of Stidham. "Thought I would check on what the arrival time is currently for majors in the rangers when they are not in deployed status."

"Bringle, I thought we agreed on 0900 for this meeting," shot back Stidham. He was beginning to remember the many annoying traits that had been deposited into one single body when they made the man sitting there.

"Well, you never accepted or declined my invitation, so I just adjusted fire." Bringle chuckled as he realized that he had gotten one over on his longtime acquaintance. Even though they had never developed that brotherhood-of-arms feeling common to many who plied their trade, he knew that Stidham had always held him at arm's length in spite of their shared experiences. He knew that, for this he had some resentment. But right now they needed to get down to business.

"If I accept, what exactly am I accepting?" quizzed Stidham as he walked around the desk and took the seat behind it. With this body maneuver, he hoped to gain control of the direction of the meeting. However, he increasingly knew he was going to accept the offer, whatever it held.

Bringle looked very nonchalant as he opened the bidding with "Well, for starters, you would get to select your all-star team of men. I know this would not be a standard ranger mission for a single team. I thought maybe three full teams to pull this off."

Stidham felt himself take the bait. "Now you and I both know this can't be done with three six-man teams. It will take at least four teams and one for backup. But I have done some preliminary work and have invited eight of the best to come here ostensibly as cadre for the school. I don't foresee any of them being reluctant to go."

Bringle nodded and paused before adding, "You know this is not a piece-of-cake mission. But I do believe it can be done by a highly motivated, well-trained force. Now let me see what you have there." Stidham shoved the copies of the personnel requisitions toward him. Bringle quickly scanned through them and smiled. "I see some old acquaintances here. I do believe they are all single men. Probably it would be a good thing to keep that going for the rest of the team."

There was no response from Stidham, but he had just been given a vital bit of information about this mission. There was a very good chance that people were not coming back. "I assume you think this is heavily guarded." He indicated the compound on the top photo. This was not a question but a statement.

"Bringle, I need to know just what you propose to do with those photos." Stidham stared at him through hard eyes, trying to determine if he could put faith in this man who had made a career of shady to dark operations and for whom the obvious was rarely the truth.

"Well, I propose that we go get these boys out of that place. Of course, it won't be these boys, but we'll make our move when there are some of our boys there. I think we take a team of thirty-two men in, and we plan for all or none." There, Bringle had laid out his proposal.

Stidham was ready and fired back at him, "Now let's get this clear. There is no we. This is my mission, my command, and definitely my neck. You will be an advisor and participate in planning, but I am not taking you with me. As you said, you have been out of the field for some time. We do this as military, or I don't go. How long do you think to get my team assembled? The military in CONUS seems to have achieved a full-ahead, slow pace on these requisitions."

Quickly, Bringle scooped up the papers from the desk. Hiding the sting of Stidham's refusal to have him on the mission, he resolved to show the military man that he could accomplish things within the labyrinthine system in which they both labored. "Can you get me an office with a phone for a bit?" he jauntily asked.

Stidham stood and escorted him next door, where a vacant full colonel's office awaited the arrival of the division HQs. "Would these humble digs be below your comfort level?" asked Stidham as he remembered the conditions they had both endured while deployed in the theatre of SEA (Southeast Asia).

"I'll make do with what I have," Bringle shot back at him as he thought about the large office he inhabited these days in the area of Foggy Bottom. "Just give me a little time."

Stidham, glad to be free of visitor for a short time, sat at his desk. He pulled a legal pad from the drawer and began to figure. He pulled the photos from the safe and began to inspect the area. Slowly he began to develop a plan for getting what he had already come to think of as "his people" into the area. Soon he was running to the cartographer's office with a request for maps of the surrounding area.

After two hours, he was startled when Bringle, without knocking on the door, returned to the office. He was obviously pleased with the results he had achieved with the use of the phone. All eight have been approved for immediate transfer. They should begin arriving here next week. Upstairs in the office of the MILPO, Ms. Vickie Cross laid down the WATTS line phone she had just heard the news from ARPERCEN (Army Personnel Center) upon. She mumbled to herself, "Now how did he do that?" She had been informed that the eight personnel whose requisition forms were still going through her process before beginning to seek transfer approval had just been approved.

She decided that she needed to go for a little walk. She found herself headed for the office that had recently been assigned to a new arrival, a Maj. William Stidham. She decided that he would have to be counseled about using the chain of command. Imagine her surprise, when she saw Colonel Albright in the hall heading for her.

Albright, the rear-detachment commander of the division who had been keeping the proverbial low profile, was visibly upset. "You are about to receive some personnel transactions for the prototype ranger school from higher headquarters. These were approved at echelons much above my head. We have been instructed to make sure that all needs of this school are dealt with favorably."

Noticing the paleness of his complexion, Ms. Cross, whispered to him, "I have received VOCO orders for eight personnel already. But, sir, I need to tell you the requisitions are still in my office being checked for thoroughness and—"

Albright quickly interceded, "Believe me, they are quite thoroughly prepared. If he has further needs, ensure that they go through immediately. My career cannot stand too much of this level of scrutiny."

Back in the office of Major Stidham, the conversation had moved on to the additional team members. Several times back and forth about the makeup followed as the two men exchanged ideas. Both had worked with some of the finest special operations soldiers in the army and were excited to compose a team. The outcome had finally been what Stidham wanted—thirty-two men. Bringle asked for names. They finally agreed upon twenty-eight.

At this juncture, inspiration struck Bringle like a bolt of lightning from the blue.

"OK, you get the twenty-eight. But I get four. Not operatives from the agency but fresh faces from here on post. We go to the TRADOC command here on post and pick up four who are about to graduate basic training. We have them licensed for M151a1 one-fourth tons (Jeeps) and two and a half tons (deuce and a half) before they finish basic. Then we give them a quick commo course on the duties of the RTO, throw in jump school—which they are very good at here—and then we use the mission training as their introduction to ranger operations, and presto, you have fulfilled your obligation here to develop and test a school. We have accomplished our training mission and have a fully functional team ready for deployment." When Bringle had finished, Stidham simply looked at him. Then he threw his hands up in the air.

"You expect me to take rookies, and I mean raw rookies on the most important mission of my career? And to cover it up by acting like I have given them the in-depth training they would need to go out in the ranger world and survive?" Stidham was almost shaking. He was so furious by the time he had gotten this out.

Bringle simply looked at him and asked the $64,000 question. "Have you thought about the endgame? How are we going to explain to our nation that we went and got these heroes from their cells, but we have these twenty-eight camera-shy rangers who don't want their pictures taken? What better than these four fresh faces to appear with them, we suddenly have a new group of heroes?"

Stidham said, "You mean you want me to take four raw rookies on this mission? They will not only be in danger, but they will also endanger my team. Absolutely no way. Not happening on my watch. I will not allow it."

Bringle just looked at him with his best Cheshire-cat look and said, "Aren't you the guy who says he can teach anyone ranger skills? Isn't that what a ranger school does?"

Stidham knew when he was not going to win and stacked arms. Hoping to at least win some concessions, he thought for a moment. "Well, I insist that I get to select the candidates."

Bringle handed him a list. "As long as they meet the requirements, you pick who you want." Bringle stared over the rim of his glasses as Stidham studied the list. "I don't know about this GT score on the ASVAB. I've never required any score. Always thought we would run off some of the ones who could make it."

"Think about it," Bringle replied. "These guys are going to be the public face of this operation if we pull this off. They have to be able to think and sell themselves to the press. This is very important."

Stidham couldn't help but point out the last requirement. "Sounds like someone doesn't think we will pull this off after all." He impishly pointed at the last requirement. "No living immediate family."

Bringle replied cheerfully, "We just don't want the family becoming the story when they get back home. We want it to be about them and, of course, the school that prepared them for this."

Stidham slowly shook his head. He knew that there was something flawed about the mission he was about to embark upon, but he didn't know how to put his finger on it. Certainly, it would not be the first time he had put his life on the line for his country, but something was there in the back of his mind saying "look at me." He just couldn't quite see it.

He decided he needed to get on with the planning. He went to Campbell Army Airfield, which, due to the absence of the 101st, was largely unused at the time. He was able to identify appropriate space for the team to quarter, and the training facilities for the jump school were up-to-date and being used. The cadre of the facility would be a huge asset to get the new troops trained. After meeting with the commandant of the school, he began to feel better about the state of affairs he was paddling upstream against.

Returning to his office, he found Bringle once again in the adjoining office. "I thought I would do some preliminary checking on personnel." The agency man grinned slyly and handed him a list of names. "These are the fourteen candidates taking BCT (basic combat training) currently in their sixth through eighth week.

They will all have graduated in two weeks. They meet all the qualifications on the list. Believe me, they are the only ones on this post who do."

Stidham accepted the list. He realized that the BCT command at Ft. Campbell was composed of two brigades. He also knew that training cycles were staggered so that every week there was a graduating class. That was about the extent of his knowledge. "I guess you found a shortcut to take to this point. I know you didn't go through the records manually." His statement while reassuring to Bringle that he might accept the list also meant he wanted to know the method used to arrive at it.

Bringle quickly explained that the army had implemented a program known as the Leadership Identification Program, where every member of every company was rated by their peers during the fifth week of BCT. Those who rated highest were notified and promised promotion to E-2 upon graduation. Bringle had simply gone to Second Brigade headquarters and gotten the list by who knew what process and come up with a manageable sample of candidates. He had then compared his list of requirements to this list, knocking out all but the fourteen soldiers.

Stidham thought about this for a few seconds and then questioned, "How many do you think will turn us down? If I were in their shoes, I don't know if I would volunteer for this."

"Not having second thoughts, are we?" responded Bringle.

"No, just wondering if we can connect across the generation gap, I guess." Stidham was not even thinking about the mission as he was trying to imagine how to approach these young men who were going to be asked to volunteer for what would be an extremely dangerous undertaking. He knew that his approach would be crucial if any of them accepted.

"Well, you're a leader, and they have been identified as leaders in their own way." Bringle's reasoning while not comforting did provide a glimmer of hope to Stidham. He thought possibly the key could be their shared interest. He imagined that finding those shared areas would involve more than merely being leaders.

"Did you make arrangements to interview these young fellows while you were over there?" Stidham asked as Bringle noted the pensiveness of the military man's mood.

"No, I thought you would want to set that schedule." Bringle did not add that this would be time-consuming and boring to him. He much preferred working alone and in the darker regions to more closely guard his secrets. Besides, this would give Stidham the appearance of control, which Bringle had already identified as one of the keys to keeping this train on the track.

Stidham looked at the list again and said, "Well, I would want First Sergeant VunCanon to sit in on these chats. He should be here next week. I am going to need some time to take care of accommodations for the rest of the team, coordinate their arrivals, get them met and settled, get the logistics of our work set up, make sure we have beans, bullets, and beds for everyone, and it might even be nice to make sure that we have a plan to pay all hands occasionally. I guess what I'm saying is that for a few days you may want to keep a low profile."

Bringle looked at him, winked, and said, "I was just about to tell you that my presence has been requested by my bosses in DC. They just can't seem to keep the wheels on the ground when I'm not there. I will be in Washington for the balance of the week. Give my regards to your excellent choices for your team personnel as they arrive. I know they will be sorry they missed me. If you need me, I will call you." With that, the agency man stood and was quickly out the door.

Preseason Week 2

Stidham grabbed his hat, headed out the door, and started to make his rounds.

His first stop was the division G-1 shop, which, like much of the post, was being manned by civilians who were hearing that the military component of the division was probably coming home soon. Since this was the first stop for incoming soldiers, Stidham realized that making his presence known would probably debur several thorny issues when his handpicked unit began arriving.

Walking into the office, he had almost asked for the acting S-1 when the figure ahead of him in line assumed its human form and enveloped him in a great bear hug. Gasping for air and desperately feeling for broken ribs, he was able to gasp. "Good afternoon, Top. I didn't expect you here until Friday." Regaining his composure, he asked, "Getting your welcome packet?"

First Sgt. David VunCanon grinned and said, "Well, some of us were just sitting around, getting bored, and your lovely summons came. We thought you must be in desperate shape to summons us from the scrap heap, so we had better get here before they discovered the error of their ways and cancelled these." He waved several sheets of paper in the air, which Stidham assumed were his orders.

"Well, Top, let's get you processed in, and we can begin setting up our little experimental school. It'll be nice having an extra set of hands to get everything set up for a few days." Stidham was already thinking of how to divide the monstrous to-do list between them, knowing that the most dependable senior NCO in the army had just dropped into his lap for three days of unplanned and unexpected assistance, which was indeed a godsend.

"Sir, your hearing getting bad?" quizzed the first sergeant. "I said we were sitting around." For the first time, Stidham looked around the office, and several others who were there assumed reality for him rather than just figures who were being processed as personnel. There was Capt. Roger Jamison, First Lt. Sam Abramson, Sgt. First Class Lev Goldman, and Sgt. First Class Herman DeWitt. All were now crowding around him and leaving the various stations where they had been mulling over the wisdom of the army in uprooting them from relatively recent assignments to send them to another post without notice. They were all immensely relieved to spot Major Stidham and knew that if he were involved in this madness of musical chair assignments, there was a good reason, and they would know what it was when he was allowed to tell them.

For his part, Stidham was beginning to realize that he had acquired five key members of his school staff four days early; and given the daunting task ahead of them, he was already planning how to take full advantage of their presence. He had just had his hand in this poker game enhanced, and he was ready to press his luck.

"Let's get you guys processed into post and settled into quarters, and then we can discuss what we have to do to get this place rocking," Stidham enthused. Once again, he went around the room, greeting each man and thanking them individually for their enthusiastic response to getting their orders and coming on such short notice. He finished with Sergeant First Class DeWitt, who was furthest along in his in-processing of the group.

"Sir, I'll have this little ole thing knocked out by this afternoon," DeWitt chirped. "I'll be ready to help you in the morning second thing." He grinned, and Stidham knew that the hard physical training necessary to perform the ranger's regimen had been neither forgotten nor neglected. A glimmer of excitement ran through him as he realized that a gigantic step had been taken in his grand experiment, and he suddenly knew that he had unquestioning allies aligned with him in this effort.

"Anyone who is interested, let's have dinner at the NCO club at 1930. We can catch up on everybody then." Stidham extended an invitation for which refusal was not an option. These men had been in the military long enough to know the difference in an invitation and a summon. Besides, they all liked the major and had no intention of letting him down. They would all be there.

That evening, promptly at 1900, a group of six combat-hardened veterans met at the NCO club. They had all done at least one tour in the Nam and had all served with Stidham for at least one tour. The conversation quickly turned to what the purpose of their being at Ft. Campbell could be. Captain Jamison was first to speak. "Whatever any of you know about this is more than I do," he started off, "career manager at DA just told me last week that I was good at Ft. Bragg for the next three years. They were going to move me to corps staff after a year with the jumpers. Apparently, this trumps DA."

They went around the table, each telling what they had been doing since coming back to "the world." They didn't even give any thought to how they had accepted that Vietnam was a different place than the rest of the world. They were so engrossed in catching up with one another that they failed to notice Major Stidham walking in at 1915. He was at the table when they first saw him.

The first to notice him was First Sergeant VunCanon, who quickly called the group to attention.

"At ease," responded Stidham while secretly appreciative of the respect being shown him. He knew that he had to get this evening on a positive track. He quickly continued, "I'm sure you are all wondering what it is that is bringing you to this lovely neck of the woods. Well, we have been selected as cadre for the prototype ranger school being developed." He went on to explain that three such projects were being developed and that the army would select what they liked from all three and consolidate the school into a single location. He further explained that each would play an integral part in the development of this project and how much it meant to him that they had expedited their arrivals so they could be here early to assist with the logistics of getting everything established in time for students.

Sergeant First Class DeWitt was first to speak when the major had finished. "Don't know if I would have been in such a hurry if I knew I was coming to school." He pretty much spoke for the group. There were nods around the table.

Stidham knew he was walking on eggshells. He glanced around the room. "I don't see what the difference is. We have run a school for all these years in Nam. It was just on the ground. For the first time, we get to teach the lads coming to us without real bullets whizzing around them. This seems better to me—for them and for me. They can make a mistake, and I know that everyone of us made mistakes when we were learning, and by the way, I believe that the learning will work both ways here. I promise that the learning will be hands-on and very limited to classroom. Notice that is a singular word. We will have only one classroom."

The men looked around somewhat sheepishly. Finally, First Sergeant VunCanon broke the stillness with the observation. "Men, I've been in a lot of tough places with the major, and he always got me out. If he needs me here, I owe it to him to give my best effort here. Major, it may sound like kiss-up time, but I'm with you all the way. Oh, I forgot that's what they say down at Bragg, so then let's say lead the way. Sir, I'm with you."

Stidham was proud of these men. All had fought hard for their country, and all were committed to the army as a way of life, but now he knew this inner corps was also committed to follow him. This was the battle he had feared from the beginning, and he had won. His fears were laid aside.

At about the time all this was concluding, the arrival of their dinners precluded any further conversation as they hastily began preparations for devouring the delicacies placed before them. Silence other than the rattle of utensils reigned. After twenty minutes, Captain Jamison looked at the major and remarked, "I was wondering if you could share with us assignments, and also, are we the entire staff of the school, or are there more coming?"

Stidham took a swallow of the sweet tea before him, nodded, and said, "A fair question, Captain. I'll address these separately. First, you are not the entire staff. We will have approximately twenty-eight individuals on the payroll when everyone is here. I think most of you will know most of those who will be joining us. Secondly, I would like to wait until the entire staff is assembled to discuss specifics of personnel roles. For the next few days, I will ask each of you to do certain things, but these taskings do not necessarily reflect final assignments. At a more appropriate time, I will go over the names with you of the remaining members who are being assigned, and we will discuss specific team duties." As he looked around the room, there were nods and smiles as each man considered his answer.

"Sir, could you tell us the rank structure?" pressed the captain.

Stidham looked directly at him and replied, "If all the personnel who have been requested accept the assignment, the rank structure will be as follows: captains (two), first lieutenant (2) both are expected to be promoted soon, first sergeant (1), first-class sergeant (4), staff sergeant (8), sergeant (10), specialist 4 (1). As much as possible, you will function in the traditional six-man team. There will be no headquarters element other than myself and the first sergeant. I prefer having each of you assigned to a team. Most of the officers and senior NCOs will receive additional duty assignments to help with staff functions, but these will be spread out and shared as equitably as possible. Keep in mind that we will have a very small class of trainees, at least in this first batch. They will be the focus of all our attention as we prepare them to survive and prosper on the battlefield."

Stidham rose from his seat and told the men, "We have a very serious task ahead of us. I asked you to come because you are some of the finest men I have had the pleasure to serve with. You were requested by me personally, or you wouldn't be here. Part of what I like about you is that you are not yes-men. You have the gumption to tell me when things are not right. Just remember you know what right looks like. If you bring me a problem, I expect that you bring at least a proposed solution, if not multiple solutions to the issue." He let these words sink in for a few moments and then continued, "Tomorrow at 0800 in my office. First Sergeant, would you walk to my car with me?"

As he and VunCanon moved to the door, he nodded to the much taller man and said, "There are a couple of things I need your help with right away."

VunCanon nodded and said, "I didn't think I was out here for the fresh air. What can I do, sir?"

"If you would, first thing tomorrow, meet and greet any other overachievers who may be in-processing at the G-1 shop. Help them, and let them know we need them on board ASAP. Secondly, I have a list of potential trainees in my office. I would like your input as to their suitability for this school." Stidham arrived at his vehicle as he finished the sentence. VunCanon, even though he was in civilian attire, crisply saluted.

"Sir, it will be an honor for me to do anything to get this school going. I know it means a lot to you, sir, but I think I have looked forward to the army doing this for at least eight to nine years. I know it will make better soldiers and help them live longer. Thank you, sir, for including me in this cadre." His voice trailed away as the major turned the key and accelerated out of the lot. VunCanon turned and went back in to the gathered fellows waiting for him.

They wanted to know what he could tell them of the school. When he assured them that the conversation had been about generalities, they soon drifted into soldier speak.

By 2100, they were ready when Captain Jamison informed them that he was ready to turn in. They quickly moved out of the club and found their way to the BOQ.

The next day, at 0730, Stidham opened the door to his office. Within three minutes, Jamison, Abramson, Goldman, and DeWitt had walked in as well. Stidham realized they were burning daylight, so he quickly brought the meeting to focus.

Turning to the butcher block chart paper on the easel behind him, he told the team, "I have taken the liberty of making preliminary assignments. I realize that you may not be comfortable with what I am asking you to take on today. Be aware these are tentative assignments written firmly in Jell-O." A nervous laugh went around the room. Stidham continued, "Captain Jamison, I want you to concentrate on operational issues, we will have some in-depth talks about these later. Today I would like you to interface with the folks at the airborne school. I don't have a feel for their quality. I assume it is pretty good. I would like their curriculum incorporated into our process."

Jamison nodded and said, "Sir, I'll get on this right away. This is right down my alley." It was obvious how relieved he was to be taking on responsibility. His apprehensive mood was a thing of the past.

Stidham then pointed to First Lieutenant Abramson, "If the lieutenant would be so kind, I would like him to take on a lot of the personnel issues. Of course, you will work very closely with Top on these matters. He has already gone to the G-1 shop to greet any new arrivals. He may be joining us shortly. Key areas in this shop will be assigning teams additional duties and, of course, documenting training, qualifications, and certifications for the school attendees." Stidham smiled when he saw just a trace of reticence on the face of the young lieutenant. His patience was rewarded in a second, when Abramson declared, "I knew Top in Nam. We'll get along like peas in a pod."

Stidham then looked at the remaining two E-7s. "I haven't forgotten you two hard-charging NCOs." He grinned at them. "I am going to ask that you take on the logistical functions. I have made arrangements for a barracks of sorts at Campbell Field. Lev, I understand you were permanent party here once upon a time?"

Goldman grunted, and DeWitt glanced slyly at him. "Be sure your sins will find you out. He thought no one knew about that."

Stidham went on, "We have to make arrangements for all the bread, beans, and bullets issues as well as knowing our way around to lay-on training resources when the time comes. I suggest a stop at G-4. They may have a new unit arrival packet to push us in the right direction to get a lot of things taken care of. You fellows have worked together for years, Lev. I would suggest that you talk to them at the 4 shop. Herman, you might want to start over at the field. Here is the contact guy over there." As he spoke, he produced a slip of paper with a name, phone number, and building number on it. Also he noted there was a second building number.

"Is this the barracks you spoke so highly of?" he inquired with a smile. Somehow he knew that there was a story behind the barracks. He was on his way out the door when he realized that he wasn't in the war but the states. Turning quickly, he mumbled, "Will that be all, sir?"

Stidham returned his salute and suggested, "We might all want to get moving. Herm, while you are over at the field, would you mind asking if they have a suite of offices we could use?"

The next sounds to fill the room was of four chairs scraping the floor as their occupants got to their feet, saluted, and were on their way.

"L-T, could I have a minute?" inquired Stidham before Abramson was out the door.

"Sir, if you think I won't do the job—" began the lieutenant.

Waving him to the chair he had just vacated, Stidham told him, "I have every confidence you will give your best at this. I just wanted to stress that it is vital to get the right people in here and get them functioning in areas where they are strong. We have so little time, and there is more to this than I can tell you or any of them right now. I think that you feel that S-1 is not where your interest lies as a career path. I understand that, but remember this is temporary, and besides, never say never."

"Sir, I apologize if I seemed to hesitate. I am almost overwhelmed by what you have offered me here. I promise my best efforts to accomplish what we need to do." The young lieutenant wanted to crawl into a hole. This man whom he had followed through the highlands of Vietnam for a year had to leave this room reassured that he had a loyal follower.

As Abramson rose to leave, he was met by VunCanon. "Sir, you'll be happy to know that we have a dozen over at the 1 shop in-processing. My guess is by the end of the day, everyone will have arrived. There were four there at eight, and they have trickled in ever since. Some may not complete in-processing until tomorrow, but I would be surprised if not all of them come in today."

Stidham was visually thrilled by this news and assessment. "Great news," he enthused. "Top, while you were gone, I went over some preliminary assignments. Most everyone has gone off to work on them or at least to hide from me. Could I get you and the lieutenant together to go over some personnel issues?"

"Certainly, sir," replied the first sergeant. The lieutenant was already back in his seat.

Stidham quickly brought Top up to speed on the assignments he had handed out. These were considered by the first sergeant, who said, "On a temporary basis, this is an outstanding lineup. Of course, we have additional talent in the bull pen and warming up."

"Correct." Stidham appreciated the approval of the first sergeant, who he knew would be the driving force behind the success of this operation, as he had come to consider it. He had already incorporated Bringle's proposal into his operation, for he knew without the aid of the agency man, his school would have never taken shape so quickly, and he surmised with the resources he was about to demand to train his small group.

Snapping him back to reality, the first sergeant looked somewhat anxious. "Sir, was there anything else?"

Stidham reached for the list of proposed candidates and handed it across the desk. Each man took it, studied it for a few moments, and handed it back to him. The lieutenant spoke first. "Sir, I don't believe I ever heard of any of these men."

"That's correct, Lieutenant." Stidham nodded at the young officer. "These men are all completing CBT in the next week or so."

VunCanon's mind was racing. "But, sir, I thought we would be bringing in troops who were experienced and just adding a layer on top of that experience."

The lieutenant was next. "What about their AIT (Advanced Individual Training)? These are not even basic infantrymen, and for that, matter they have not even done jump school."

"Here's the plan: We are having them licensed on quarter-ton and two-and-a-half-ton vehicles as part of CBT. Each company is required to have a certain number of these to complement the training process. When they come to us, we finish off any hour requirements they have as OJT (on the job training) and award the 63 C 10 MOSs (wheeled vehicle driver). Then we incorporate jump school into our regimen. The actual jump training will be handled by school cadre from the post. Although I'm sure any one of our team could handle that, we will be plenty busy getting everything laid on for our endeavors. Then they come out of here ready to undertake a practical mission." Stidham paused and took stock of the reactions of his two trusted coworkers.

Finally, First Sergeant VunCanon spoke quietly. "Sir, you keep making reference to a mission at the end of the school? I assumed that there would be an intense field training exercise (FTX) before we signed them off as being ready. I must say, sir, that this is sounding like something else. Could you give us more details? It's hard knowing what we are shooting at in the dark."

Stidham studied them intently. "Yes, there is an endgame here. I would prefer not to get into specifics until the entire team is assembled. Then everyone gets to hear the same story, and everyone can react as they need to. Can you live with that for twenty-four more hours?"

They both nodded. "I have made copies of their 2-1s, and they are in these packets." Once again, Stidham was handing them copies before he finished speaking. The 2-1 summarized the achievements of each man and his qualifications. "Some of these are very impressive. I think it may be helpful for you to have this also." Once again, he was handing across the desk copies of the requirements for admission that he and Bringle had established.

After several seconds, the first sergeant led off. "Sir, few if any of the enlisted men meet these GT scores, I would bet. This may be a problem for our men to deal with these." He indicated the pile of files before him.

"Top, isn't what we have always preached that we want thinkers who can react to fluid situations as they arise? Don't you think that these guys give us the best chance of getting this result?" Stidham was not being judgmental in his tone to the first sergeant, but he did want him to see his point.

"I suppose that is a better way to look at it. My glasses were fogged up there for a minute." He smiled, and Stidham knew that issue had gone to bed.

First Lieutenant Abramson, after observing this give-and-take, felt emboldened to make a point. "Sir, there are roughly 6 companies graduating CBT per week at this post, I think. You said these fourteen are all that meet these requirements? At 130 men per company, that would be about 2,300 men over a three-week period. I would have thought we would have a larger pool than this."

The major agreed and then said, "One thing skewing this is that it is late summer. Traditionally, the NG and ER (national guard and enlisted reserve) numbers are very heavy at this time of year. I understand that there are almost eight hundred guardsmen and reservists reflected in these statistics. Obviously, we did not consider them for this opportunity."

"I would hope that we can interview these candidates before we have to select from the list." This observation came from the first sergeant.

"Well, now that you mention it there is a graduation planned for tomorrow. If we don't interview the four men on the list from that cycle today, they will be moving on tomorrow." Stidham was already picking up the phone to call the S-3 at Second Brigade headquarters and was assured that the individuals needed would be at his office at 1300. They would have ample time with them individually.

"Now why don't I buy you lunch at the local bistro?" Stidham shot at them, and they all laughed. They knew they were headed for the closest mess hall.

Arriving back at his office at the headquarters at 1245, they were immediately aware of the four young men awaiting them in the hallway. The first to spot them coming in quickly called the group to "Attention." This surely made a good impression on the first sergeant. Stidham quickly responded with "At ease." Introductions were quickly made, including the drill sergeant who had escorted the trainees to their interviews.

Stidham turned to the Drill and told him, "I am sure that we can keep these young men occupied for the afternoon. I imagine you will want to see them back to barracks, but I also imagine you have some other things to do in the meantime. If you want, we will see you at about 1630."

"Yes, sir." The drill's answer was too enthusiastic for the occasion, but they all got a kick out of it, realizing it was done primarily for the benefit of the trainees who were about to display the fruits of their training to these men whom he noted were all wearing combat patches on their right sleeve and displaying CIBs and jump wings on their chests. This was all he needed to see to know he had placed them in good hands.

"Well, gentlemen, who wants to go first?" asked First Sergeant VunCanon.

"I will, First Sergeant," replied the first man in line.

"Well, come on in," Stidham responded. The four men moved into the small conference room across the hall. Stidham proceeded to tell the man as much as he could about the training opportunity that was being offered.

After about twenty-five minutes, the young man said, "Sirs", taking in both officers, "I have to tell you that if I had had this opportunity offered to me when I was joining the army. I would have jumped at it. But I have a reservation for a seat in an NSA class. I don't think I can afford to give that up. Thank you for your consideration, but I think I'll pass."

With that, he was given permission to depart. Stidham turned to Abramson. "Young man, I think it will go better if you take the lead on this one. We may be experiencing a generation gap here." Abramson reluctantly acquiesced.

"Feel free to jump in at any time," he told both the older men and rose to retrieve the next candidate. So their afternoon went until at 1615, the final prospective student had turned them down.

"I'm feeling old and rejected." Stidham couldn't help but agree with the lieutenant's assessment. But he needed to keep his positive approach.

"We'll all get better with practice," he opined. "Rome wasn't built in a day, so my dad used to tell me."

First Sergeant VunCanon looked pensively at the door where the four young recruits had disappeared with their drill sergeant who, of course, had arrived fifteen minutes before the instructed time. He was a professional and portrayed it in all his actions. "I think we had all better think about our contributions to this series of interviews," he said with a tone that made them all stop and look at him. "Something we are doing is not connecting with these young men. I don't know exactly what it is, but we need to find out."

Stidham looked at both men. "Well, I have arranged for the other ten to see us tomorrow. We will have the six from the week 7 companies in the morning and the other four from week 6 companies in the afternoon. Gentlemen, I have to catch up with my other troops, so please excuse me."

First Sergeant VunCanon, already on his feet, called the room to attention. They were quickly placed at ease by Stidham. VunCanon continued to his back, "I am going to check on my new arrivals." With that, he was out the door and on his way.

First Lieutenant Abramson sat for a moment, thinking about the foiled interviews. He could not remember in the year he had spent in South Vietnam, or very close by, ever having heard anyone tell Major Stidham the word "no." He walked across the hall and looked at the hastily prepared distribution center that the S-4 guys had procured from the triple S-C shop on post and thought, *I bet they are about to become very well-known down there.*

In the slot labeled S-1, he found that eight additional soldiers had already finished in-processing and their 201 files were lying there waiting for him. On the top were two of particular interest to him—the first was for Capt. (P) Thurman Mizell, and the second for First Lt. Anthony Scandretti.

Quickly returning to the conference room, he scanned the 201 files. His first reaction to Mizell's file was that he wouldn't be here long, and then the thought occurred to him, unless Stidham was also carrying a P after his rank. Then there were possibilities he had not considered. He leafed through Scandretti's file, noting that he had spent a year in Vietnam right after his own return, so that had been Stidham's connection to him. He realized it was rare for two men's time in country to exactly coincide.

He noticed that the final six months of tour had been spent in the first of the fifth Regimental HQs as BN S-1. He was beginning to feel better. Digging deeper into the pile, he noticed that also having arrived was Sgt. First Class Larry McCord, an experienced ranger NCO, and Sgt. First Class Walter Taylor, also an experienced ranger. *Hmm,* he thought to himself, *I can see possibly four teams coming from this.* He began putting into place his recommendations to Stidham just in case he was asked. He had learned long ago to anticipate what his leader would require of him, and he usually managed to exceed those expectations when given time to anticipate. He planned to be ahead this day.

A little after 1800, he saw Stidham coming down the hall. "Sir, I have received 201 files for eight more personnel." He quickly brought the major up to date on those files. This was accomplished in little time due to the major's knowledge of the men involved. Upon the completion of the report, the major thanked him for his persistence in getting through this and informed him that effective tomorrow, they would be working from an old World War II barracks that they would be converting into office space. The location was over at Campbell Army Airfield, next to the barracks they had procured for the troops.

Stidham had already heard the news from First Sergeant VunCanon but was still appreciative of the gung-ho attitude from the young lieutenant. He was working well beyond the normal amount, and he was enthusiastically going about a task he had admitted was not his favorite.

Stidham had several details to clean up. He was wrapped up by 2100 and headed to his quarters. As he was leaving the HQs building, he noticed that Goldman and DeWitt were headed his way. He thanked them for the work they had done on getting the buildings released to them. "Piece of cake," Goldman remarked.

"Well, tomorrow we begin inhabiting them." Stidham let the pride he felt in all that had been accomplished in less than a week creep into his voice. "I think our team is really starting to click. We have to keep our forward lean, and everything will be great," he assessed.

The next morning, he decided to dispense with the three miles he normally put in every Friday. Instead, he walked into the building being converted from barracks to office space at 0600. He was thinking that he would get an early start on the items he had determined to accomplish today. It was encouraging to see that Goldman and DeWitt had already started moving office furniture into the vacant building. Upon closer inspection, he noticed two shapes in the back of the two-and-a-half-ton truck backed up to the main entrance of the building. Moving to speak to them, he realized that Sergeant First Class McCord and Sergeant First Class Taylor had voluntarily joined their fellow first-class sergeants in making this the team's home.

"Good morning, men," he boomed in his officer's best voice. "Glad to see you gentlemen are no longer on the gravy train out at Ft. Carson. Welcome to Campbell."

Shucking the gloves they had on their hands for protection, the two old friends of the major rushed to salute and then enthusiastically started to ask a dozen questions without waiting for answers to any of them. "Fellows, we told you the major will be conducting a briefing for all team members at 0800. He hasn't told any of us anything except to expect to work hard and be underpaid." DeWitt laughed. "So far he has lived up to his word."

Goldman, after the banter of the welcome, sidled over to the side of Stidham and very quietly asked, "Sir, could I ask you about something?"

"Certainly," replied Stidham. "What's on your mind?"

"You may not be aware of this, but after you left the unit in Nam, Brown and Younts were brought up on charges of undue cruelty in dealing with some of our host nation civilians. I don't know if you are aware of this or not. They were both reduced in rank from 5 to 4. When I saw them in-processing, I noticed that Brown had received his stripe back."

Stidham frowned and looked directly into Goldman's eyes. "I was aware of the charges. They both contacted me for statements of character during their hearings. They both are technically among the best I have ever seen. Our guys don't have to learn everything from them, but I do believe they have earned the right to a second chance."

"Thank you, sir." Goldman was finished with the effort, but in his mind, he had not achieved the level of forgiveness that he had heard from the major. This was a grave concern for him, and he resolved to watch these two carefully for any sign that they were not exhibiting the best attitudes toward the young men they would be training.

Stidham, upon reflecting on DeWitt's comments, was startled that this was DeWitt's assessment of his first hours. But after pausing to think about it, he realized that it was given in good humor and that it was true. He remembered an old officer's basic infantry instructor telling him that if a soldier was complaining about something trivial, he was generally pretty happy, and how true he had found this axiom to be throughout his career.

Walking in to the old building, he was drawn into what had once been a cadre room just inside the building. Looking in, he was surprised to see the few items he had unpacked at the HQs office he had recently inhabited. His men had already affected his move. He was more and more feeling how well his selections were working out. Taking a seat, he picked up the phone and was amazed to get a dial tone. These guys were really good.

At 0700, he was interrupted by a knock on his door. Glancing up, he saw First Sergeant VunCanon standing at attention. "Sir, the men are assembled. I know you were planning on them being here at 0800, but we have those interviews. I thought we might get at least some of the organizational stuff out of the way and give these guys some direction to get them going."

"Top, give me two minutes. If you have anything to start off, go ahead and put it out." Stidham was prepared, but he wanted to give the men the hint that they might be ahead of him ever so slightly. He understood what a boost this would be for their morale.

"We will be in the platoon bay, up top." The first sergeant turned and was gone. In less than fifteen seconds, he was up the stairs and into the large platoon bay. Quickly calling the men to attention, he began with roll call and moved on to duty rosters, chow halls parking permits, walking-around orders, and the other five things he had on his list.

Stidham stood at the foot of the stairs, listening to this efficient NCO going about his business, and said a little prayer under his breath. "Lord, please help me lead these men to the best of the ability you have blessed me with. Help me build character and accomplish goals that will be set for us. May all the glory go to you." He heard the first sergeant begin to wind up his presentation, for VunCanon, like most senior NCOs, had long ago perfected the art of brevity.

As he reached the top of the stairs, he heard the booming voice of Taylor ring out. "Attention!"

Striding to the hastily assembled podium, he turned and looked for a moment at his command. He felt the thrill of pride shoot through him. He thought, *These men are the very best I have ever served with. What an honor to get them all together.* "At ease, and take your seats." He never looked at the bright yellow legal pad he held in his hand as he began to speak. "We have been selected to begin a prototype US Army Ranger School here at Ft. Campbell," he intoned. Warming to the topic, he went on to describe how the school would be evaluated along with the other prototypes being developed at approximately the same time as theirs. He went over the honor that they had been paid by the ranger hierarchy to be in this position. After fifteen minutes, he paused, looked them over, and said, "Any questions?"

"Sir"—Captain (P) Mizell had taken his feet—"can you tell us the rank structure and manning plan for this?"

Grinning at the captain, Stidham nodded. Growing deadly serious, he informed them, "The plan as it exists in today's world is that there will be a real-life problem at the end of our cycle. This mission is currently classified, but I can tell you it is extremely dangerous. I can also tell you that the rewards for pulling it off are exceptional. It could result in the saving of several servicemen's lives." He paused to let the seriousness of this message sink in. "Continuing," he started up again, "if any of you are hesitant to undertake this, I know that you have all done your duty to your country. You will be released and returned to your previous unit. I am sorry, but that decision must be made now. If you remain in this room at 0730"—he glanced at the clock behind him, noting it said 0728—"then you are considered to have volunteered. I am serious. No hard feelings and no retribution, if you are unable to continue. If you are still here at 0730, then we will begin making assignments and discussing those details we can divulge. Since everyone here has at least a secret clearance, once we have a commitment to the mission, we can begin to tell you details. You will not get a full mission brief today. We are quite a way from that." He stopped and sat down.

The seconds ticked off painfully slowly from the old clock on the barracks wall. When it reached 0730, Stidham stood and looked around the room. "I am humbled that every one of you elected to stay. I will strive to justify your faith in me as a leader from now on. Who's ready for assignments?"

Sergeant First Class DeWitt brought up the butcher block and easel that had been brought over from the previous home of the unit. When the major flipped the covering front sheet, he was amazed to see the outlined schematic of a unit wiring diagram. He realized that First Lieutenant Abramson had listened very well. The assignments were exactly as he would have made them. At the top, of course, was the major and with him the first sergeant. Immediately below the first sergeant was Sgt. Gibby Gibson. "For those of you who don't know Sergeant Gibson. He is the young man sitting on the front row." Stidham indicated a lanky young man who rose so that all could see him. "He is a magician with requisitions," Stidham continued. "His motto, he has always told me, is 'You have not because you ask not.' Now let me emphasize, that doesn't mean a verbal asking, but put it on paper, and I think he will get it." Stidham then went on to the four six-man ranger teams identified. Team 1 led by Captain (P) Mizell and NCOIC Sergeant

First Class Goldman, Team 2 led by Captain Jamison and NCOIC Sergeant First Class McCord, Team 3 led by First Lt. Anthony Scandretti and Sergeant First Class DeWitt, and finally team 4 led by First Lieutenant Abramson and NCOIC Sergeant First Class Taylor. "Now some of you have been asked to assume certain duties already. This schematic does not release you from those duties but gives you functions to keep you gainfully employed should you run out of anything to do to keep busy." Stidham laughed, and the whole room chuckled as the tension had been broken by the revelation of the teams and righteous look of the slim HQs depicted on the butcher block.

"I am going to turn you over to your team leaders except that First Lieutenant Abramson, Top, and I have appointments with a group of perspective students."

As Stidham started toward the back of the room, First Sergeant VunCanon bellowed, "Attention!"

"Carry on!" instantly came Stidham's response. The men immediately began to break up into teams as indicated by the butcher block.

Stidham glanced at his watch as he and his team of interviewers headed for the steps at the back of the room. He noticed that it was 0750. The first sergeant noticed, gave him a wink, and a thumbs-up signal. "Sir, you were awesome, not a single defection," the older NCO enthused. "I believe we are on the right track."

"Let's hope so." Stidham was painfully aware that he had been dealing with a hand-selected group of men with whom he had shared the rigors of a combat zone. Even so, not all of them had shared experiences with one another. The group of young men waiting at the front of the building seemed to him unlikely to have needed to shave before coming over. Once again, pleasantries were exchanged with the drill sergeant who had brought the recruits over. The drill was informed that he would need to pick up his half dozen charges at about 1130.

Once again, the men were called in one at a time. Again, the school was explained, and it was emphasized that this was a brand-new, unique opportunity they were being presented. Again, Stidham and VunCanon did most of the talking. By 1130, Pvl James Wiznewski had become their first student. Once again, five others had respectfully declined the invitation. "So many songs by the band and so few dancers," ruefully observed the first sergeant.

When the drill sergeant returned to take control of his detail, he was instructed about Wiznewski and given permission to return them to their units. Abramson had already begun the personnel requisition form that would be needed. He would finish it that afternoon. Stidham was growing exasperated at the lack of progress in recruiting candidates for the school. He looked at the other members of his hiring team and said, "We have until 1300 to come up with what we are doing wrong and correct it. We need students. Let's go to the mess hall and see if we can come up with any solutions." Grabbing his black beret, he headed for the door.

Only a block away, the walk gave them time to get a breath of fresh air as the head count greeted them. They were impressed by the efficiency of Taylor and/or DeWitt as they noted the sergeant held a unit head-count sheet for their unit, not just a visitor's count. Stidham made sure to point out this to the two men with him. "I'll make sure to mention it on their NCO ERs." First Sergeant VunCanon was only half-joking as he mentioned the ever-present evaluation tool that everyone above the rank of E-4 in the army was constantly aware.

As they moved through the serving line, receiving their portions from the mess staff, they wondered what grade of chow hall they had chanced upon. Sitting down in officer's country, their questions were soon answered. The chow was very good. As he cut into his steak, First Lieutenant Abramson spoke for the first time since the last interview had concluded, "Sir, could I make a suggestion about the interviews?" He spoke somewhat hesitantly for good reason as they all understood when Stidham nodded and added, "I wish you would."

"Well, sir, I don't think we are doing anything wrong with the information we are giving them, but I notice that you and Top are doing most of the presentation. At first, I was fine with that, but, sir, I have to notice that Wiz (he had already nicknamed Wiznewski) is twenty-three years old and has finished college. The others were no more than eighteen to nineteen years old, all seem above average intelligence, but they are very young. Sir—"

Before he could go further, Stidham smiled and interrupted, "Excuse me, young man," he started. "I believe I see your point. We have a generation gap here, don't we?"

"Well, sir, I don't think it's just between Wiz and these other young men." The lieutenant was warming up.

"Go on, "urged Stidham.

"Well, sir, if you would allow it, on the next interview would you allow me to do more of the talking and explaining. Not that what you and Top are saying is wrong. I just think sometimes it goes over better coming from someone closer to them in age." There he had said it. He looked up bleakly, wondering if he had just ended his military career this soon after getting it started.

First Sergeant VunCanon, the most senior by age of the group, laughed and clapped the lieutenant on the shoulder. "I was never happier to be called an old fogie. But you are right. We have to try something. Sir, I say we have had ten shots at it with one hit. Let's at least give the lieutenant one shot. We've got to go down swinging."

"I see what you mean," mused Stidham. "This afternoon's first interview is yours, Lieutenant. We will be there to support you, but unless you or the interviewee asks us a direct question, all commo will come from you. We'll see how it goes."

The lieutenant thought for a second and then added one more proposal, "Sir, I would like to interview Woodie Foster first out of this group. I feel like he is a ranger waiting to happen."

"May I ask why?" Stidham was surprised by this request. Up until this point, they had allowed the candidates to order themselves.

"Well, sir, he's nineteen years old from rural Colorado. He has hunted and fished all his life. I think he is perfect for us. But I also think that if we click with him, he will go out and recruit the others for us with his enthusiasm. By the time we talk to them, we just have to seal the deal." Stidham studied the lieutenant for several moments.

"And here I thought you were just another pretty face." The world suddenly grew brighter. He felt that they had solved the recruiting mystery. "Just out of curiosity, Lieutenant, where did you become so knowledgeable of the psychology of recruiting?"

"Sir, I was recruited by a master sergeant named Homer Dick. He taught me more than just to go to OCS, I guess." Stidham knew there was more to it than that, however. He hadn't mentioned a four-year degree in psychology from Vanderbilt University.

As they departed the chow hall, Stidham felt almost like jogging back to their new office/barracks. He was enthused by their prospects.

Arriving back at the office, they once again found a drill sergeant with four young recruits waiting for them. Stidham assured the drill that his detail was in good hands and asked him to return at 1600. The drill was happy to have some time to take care of personal business.

Stidham introduced the team to the trainees. While Abramson informed them of the details of what they would be doing, Stidham and VunCanon went into the office. Stidham immediately began to rearrange the furniture, first pulling his chair from behind the desk and then placing the chairs into a circle. Catching on, VunCanon was able to assist before the lieutenant, escorted by young Private Foster, entered the room. Foster quickly spotted Major Stidham, saluted, and reported, "Sir, Private Foster, reporting as requested."

Stidham looked over at Abramson and then replied, "At ease, soldier. Have a seat. Lieutenant Abramson, would you be so kind as to explain what we have to offer this gentleman?"

Abramson, for his part, vigorously nodded and began to tell the story of the prototype ranger school to be set up here and the opportunities inherent in coming from this background. He never mentioned the military as a career, the glamor or the glory. He simply talked about mission and core values that were shared not only by those in this room but also by all who wore the ranger patch. He talked about the camaraderie and the pride of belonging. He stressed that this wasn't just about a school but a commitment to a way of life, that the dangers of any mission assigned the rangers was usually great and that he could tell him there would be a real-life mission at the close of school.

After about ten minutes, he realized the passion with which he had spoken and began to relax a little. Asking Foster for any questions, he wasn't surprised that he had plenty. Abramson never hesitated to turn to the older men in the room when he wasn't sure of the answers. Together they went like this for about thirty minutes.

Finally, they were finished, the flow of information coming slower. First Lieutenant Abramson, looked at the young recruit sitting beside him. He began to tell him of what he knew of his background and drew further details from him. His mother had left when he was three. Raised by his dad, who was a lover of the outdoors. A successful if not spectacular student, he had finished high school, reported to the draft board, and decided to join the army rather than wait for the draft.

After about three minutes of "This Is My Life," he turned to the lieutenant. "Sir, when will I know if I have been accepted?" The major's heart was pumping out about 180 beats per minute when he heard this.

The lieutenant simply nodded to the major and said, "I believe Major Stidham can answer that for you."

Stidham was about to jump out of his seat but managed. "Well, I believe we can offer you a seat in this first group."

Foster beamed. "Do you mean it? Man, I mean, sir, I would dearly love to do this."

First Lieutenant Abramson slipped the folder off the desk behind him and handed the forms to him. Stidham noticed that the pertinent information had already been filled in. He was really appreciating the eye for talent this young lieutenant was developing.

"I need to see a man about a dog," Stidham announced. "You two go ahead and finish up here."

First Sergeant VunCanon quickly joined him as he exited the office and headed for the latrine at the back of the building. He was feeling super. As he washed his hands, he was surprised by the first sergeant's words. "Sir, you better watch out. The lieutenant will be thinking he runs things here."

"Top, I have always taught junior officers to develop as leaders and to enhance their skills in any way I could. I don't feel threatened in any way by seeing him pull this off. Just as I would think you would take pride in seeing what the NCO's junior to you are accomplishing."

"Right, sir" came the response. "I guess I am just used to following one man. I never thought about the whole thing, I will have to get better at that as we go. I hope, sir, that you accept my apology."

"No apology necessary, Top. I appreciate that you are watching my back. That's how we have gotten this far. I want you to know that my goal is for every one of our officers to show excellence in every situation," Stidham replied.

As they were drying their hands, in came the lieutenant. "If you guys wouldn't mind, we need to stay back here a few more minutes." He looked in the mirror above the lavatory where he had begun to wash his hands. "Our number 1 recruiter will need a few minutes to sell his new passion. Particularly, since all these men are from different companies. They probably don't know one another." They continued to make small talk for a couple of minutes.

At last, the type-A personality of the two older men kicked in, and they had to move out. As they approached the group of trainees from the rear of the building, they could clearly hear Foster's voice brimming with excitement. Exactly as the lieutenant had predicted, he was doing their selling for them. The senior team members slipped into the room.

A few seconds later, they were joined by First Lieutenant Abramson and another fresh-faced young man. "Sir, may I introduce you to Pvt. Kevin Nuckles from North Carolina." Abramson went on about the exploits of Nuckles, a two-sport high school athlete, captain of the football and wrestling teams at the small high school he had attended in the piedmont area of the state. Abramson went on to explain that he had been an honor graduate, ranking eighth in a class of 143.

Nuckles quickly came to the position of attention and saluted, "Sir, Private Nuckles, reporting as ordered, sir."

Stidham responded, "At ease, Private. Please be seated. I hope you will feel glad you came and not just because you were ordered to come."

Blushing bright red, the private stammered, "No, sir, I was just reporting in as they taught us in basic, sir."

Stidham thought, *I hope we get this one. Two sentences and four sirs! He is certainly good for the ego.* After listening to the young man and the lieutenant exchange ideas about the training, Stidham was impressed. He found himself hoping they had found their third man. After about twenty-five minutes of thoughtful conversation, Nuckles turned to the major, "Sir, may I know when I will know if I have been accepted for this School?"

The major could not resist. "Got a hot date back in Carolina when you graduate?"

"Well, sir, no, sir, that is." The flustered private paused before going on, "Sir, I haven't told anyone I left back there, but I don't ever plan on going back to Smallsbury. Whether I go to this school or not, I don't intend to go back, sir." The passion of this declaration caught the three older men off-guard somewhat, for none of them had ever forgotten the roots from which they came. Stidham wondered at this in the young man before him.

"I don't mean to be personal, but may I ask why you would not return to your hometown?" The first sergeant let no inflection come into his voice as he asked the question all three had been rolling over in their heads. "Well, Top, you see, my parents split up while my brother was in Nam. No one would write to him and tell him. He was killed over there. I don't want anyone writing letters full of lies to me."

Satisfied by this answer, Stidham studied him. "You asked when you would know if you are accepted. Are you ready to make a commitment to us if we accept you?"

"Yes, sir."

Nuckles was ecstatic that he had been accepted. He had enlisted with the promise of a class in the signal corps, which would have required nine months to complete. The beautiful thing about this to Stidham was that the commo school had required a top-secret security clearance, and this had already been done. He was definitely cleared for rumor and above as he had heard others say.

Stidham was almost beside himself as he realized that he had the third man. Already, his thoughts were turning to the two men left outside the office. Could they possibly be lucky enough to get their fourth man from those two? After getting Abramson and Nuckles started on the paperwork, Stidham excused himself. He asked the first sergeant to accompany him to the common area on the upper floor. He explained to him that he had to make a phone call, but he wanted to be interrupted after ten minutes.

Picking up the phone with the WATTS access code he had been given at HQs, he slowly dialed the number on Bringle's business card. After several seconds and with much clicking and electrical exchanges, he heard the agency man on the phone. "How is it going out there?" Bringle's voice came over the connection.

"I was lonesome and needed to hear a familiar voice," Stidham shot out. "Are we making any progress on our situation?"

"I think you will be pleased by what we have. Looks like an early Christmas present from our friend Ho." Stidham knew that was all he would get from Bringle over the phone.

"I wanted you to know that we have three guinea pigs committed and two more to interview." Stidham was pleased to report. "I think you would be pleased with the progress we are making. I was wondering when we can start preliminary briefings so I can begin to tell the men why they are here. I think my song and dance routine is wearing thin on them."

"I think the Austrian will be wrapping up on this end today," Bringle informed Stidham. "I should be able to get out there by Tuesday."

Stidham now knew that Bringle was not in the country, and his guess was that he was in Paris, France, again for another round of talks. He wondered what type of cover story Bringle was using but did not dwell on it. At that moment, First

Sergeant VunCanon stuck his head in the door and pointed at his watch. Stidham realized that he had to get back to the two remaining interviews.

Quickly coming out of the office, he picked up the first sergeant's pace as they crossed the open common area. "Sir, I have to say the lieutenant sure has figured it out. It would be a shame to lose such a fine young tactical officer, but he would make a top-notch recruiter, don't you think?"

"He has convinced me," Stidham replied. They had reached Stidham's office. Abramson sat on a chair with the last two 201 files before him. Poking his head in the door, Stidham queried, "Do you think we should interview them or just let Foster and Nuckles handle it?"

With a self-effacing laugh, Abramson said, "Well, they could probably do it, but we should probably close the deal, sir."

"I see your point, Lieutenant." Stidham was feeling very pleased with the direction things were heading. He was not about to mess things up by taking the bit out of the lieutenant's mouth. He liked what he had seen up to now. The lieutenant arose and went to the door. Stepping out in the hall, he called the next name. He quickly went over the reporting procedure with the trainee and made sure he was comfortable with what he had to do. Then he led him to the door.

"Sir, I would like you to meet Pvt. Steven Ash." Abramson nodded, and the young man moved forward. Once again, the reporting procedure unfolded smoothly. It turned out that Ash had been raised in an orphanage in Mississippi and had finished high school in Tupelo. Feeling bored and not having much else to do, he had befriended the local army recruiter, who had been trying to learn the intricacies of getting fish to jump onto his hook in the waters around the area. They both come out winners according to Ash. The first sergeant spoke for the first time, wondering if there had been a guaranteed option for further training.

"Well, first sergeant, if there was, I have plumb forgotten what it might have been. Listening to those two yahoos out there, y'all seem to have something special going here. If I could, I would dearly love to sign up right now." Ash's sincerity would have melted the heart of the most cynical skeptic.

Abramson immediately leaped into the conversation, explaining the nuances of the school and the training that would be involved. After twenty minutes, Ash looked over at the major. "Sir, can you unwind him? I still want to do it, but if he talks much longer, I may change my mind." They all laughed. Abramson produced the required paperwork, and they had their fourth man.

The break between men was brief, and before 1500, Pvt. David Cansler was seated in the interview room. Cansler was a twenty-year-old who had done very well in high school graduating from Central High in Columbus, Ohio. He had enrolled at Kent State University and gotten involved with the antiwar movement on campus. Becoming disenchanted, he had dropped out of the movement and the school in March before the famous incident had occurred there. He had been very surprised at how quickly the draft board became aware of his disenrollment and sent him a letter from his friends and neighbors. Needless to say, he had found his way here. He had been very surprised to find that a good number of his basic training company were students from Kent State who were, in fact, members of the Ohio National Guard. He had been amazed at the barracks talk with these guys about their feelings toward the guard and the antiwar movement. Basic training had indeed taught him much more than combat survival and basic soldiering skills.

After listening to Abramson's spiel for twenty-five minutes, he was impressed but unmoved. He looked to Major Stidham and began choosing his words very carefully. "Sir, I am honored to have been selected for an interview, but I have excellent typing and office skills. For the past two weeks, I have been assigned to drive jeeps and a deuce and a half. I have no interest in being a truck driver. If you could use me as a unit clerk or something of that nature, I would be happy to work with you."

Stidham sat absolutely still. Here was a young man who had spent considerable time and energy working to oppose the things he stood for. Yet, sitting here in this room, he felt no animosity toward him and sensed none from the young man. The thought crossed his mind, *What a great country that we can express our differences so openly and still see our way to work together.* Choosing his words carefully, he said, "At this time, we all have to be rangers. I understand your preference of a working area. I can offer you this rigorous training, but I can't promise you that you will only work in the orderly room." Perhaps swaying him more than anything was the top-secret security clearance young Cansler had in his 201 file. He had to admit that he had been reluctant to look for someone with the office skills that were obviously, going to become extremely critical. He thought of the old axiom, "That no job is ever done until the paperwork is complete."

Abramson interjected, "Sir, if I may." Encouraged by a nod from Stidham, he continued, "I have been asked at least temporarily to undertake the S-1 functions for the school/team. If I am to be a team leader, I will certainly need someone functioning in the role we have been discussing."

Stidham nodded his acquiescence and said, "Have him assigned to the school as cadre, not student. That is, of course, Lieutenant, if this is the man you want for the job."

Quickly, Abramson reached for Cansler's hand and pronounced, "Welcome to the US Army Ranger School, Ft. Campbell, Kentucky." The ring of the title was pleasing to the men in the room.

When the paperwork had been completed, Abramson escorted the last of the trainees back to the hallway where the balance of the detail waited with the recently arrived drill sergeant who was looking sharp with his newly acquired haircut. Abramson couldn't resist. "I see how you spent at least part of your time."

"Gotta stand tall, sir" was the drill sergeant's only verbal response, but the smile on his face gave away his pleasure in looking the part he was paid to play in this man's army.

"Well, Lieutenant, do you have something you want to tell me?" Stidham inquired when the lieutenant had returned to the room.

"Yes, sir. You see, sir, I was thinking that maybe becoming the 1 was not such a bad idea, especially if I get to work with this caliber of men." Abramson chose his words carefully. He wasn't sure he had thought this all the way through, but he had certainly enjoyed his afternoon.

"Your offer is accepted," Stidham responded before there was time for any further negotiation. "Now I believe there is probably quite a bit of paperwork to be completed." He thus dismissed the junior officer.

He turned to see the dark look on the face of the first sergeant. "Sir, I must say that I have some misgivings about this last team member. He was involved in the antiwar movement less than a year ago, and here we are, opening up our training for him. What if he is a plant?"

"I thought about that, but you know what? I don't think it matters. The training should not be a deep secret. It should be above board. The mission is top secret. He has a clearance for that. This tells me his involvement in the war movement was not so deep as we might think." Stidham paused and then continued, "I think this will work to everyone's advantage. This young man apparently has become disheartened with those people who may have been leading him down a different path than we have taken, but this may be our opportunity to get him back."

VunCanon thought about this for a moment. "I have to go to my office and ponder this." With this statement, he stood, saluted, and was gone. Stidham knew he had some fences to mend with this man who he desperately needed for the day ahead.

Regular Season Begins

Week 1

Dallas 17–Philadelphia 7
Baltimore 16–San Diego 14

Woodie Foster woke up in the bunk he had made up the night before. For a moment, he lay under the sheet, trying to place where he was. He knew he was no longer in the basic training barracks he had inhabited for the previous eight weeks. There was no snoring coming from the top bunk. Glancing at the underside of the bunk, he knew no one could be there; the bunk was totally empty, no mattress or any bedding materials.

Slowly it began to come back to him. He had listened to First Lieutenant Abramson and Major Stidham and decided to throw in with them on this new project. His military career was on the upswing. He, like the other inhabitants of the room, a large platoon bay in an old World War II wooden barracks, had all been promoted to PV2 upon the completion of Combat Basic Training. This sudden influx of rank had raised their monthly pay from $124 per month to the whopping sum of $136 per month. How would he ever spend it all?

Each occupant had been given a double bunk arrangement for their sleeping accommodations. They were allowed to leave the second bunk or dismantle it as they preferred. This was, in most cases, the most free will they had been allowed to exercise since their arrival at Ft. Campbell. For the ones who had come from Ft. Polk due to the overbooking of the CBT capabilities of that post, this really represented progress. What they had yet to realize was how drafty cold and open these old buildings were in the winter. He suspected he would not be here to discover this when the cold weather of winter descended.

They had spent the past two months in the new modern barracks of the 101st Airborne Division constructed from cinderblocks in the midfifties. These buildings had been closed up tight when the division shipped out to the Nam. Now that it looked like they would be redeploying back to Ft. Campbell, the powers that be on post had ordained that a couple of rotations of basic training would get their barracks cleaned up and ready for their habitation. He felt so grateful to know that his work would be so well appreciated by the soldiers who would be benefitting from it—*not*.

Looking over to the next bunk, he spotted PV2 Kevin Nuckles, whose acquaintance he had made the previous evening. They had both been a little nervous when they were told that the trainees would be exempt from KP (kitchen patrol) for the duration of their training. PV2 James Wiznewski was still breathing the heavy breath of that final deep sleep just before the time to rise. This brought his attention to the fact that no such noise was coming from Nuckles. *Early riser*, he thought. Even further down the bay was PV2 Steven Ash. He honestly couldn't tell if he slumbered or simply awaited the sign that it was time to turn out. Turning his head to look out the window, he could tell that the predawn light was just arriving to herald a day for the group.

Unaccustomed as they were to not having loud obnoxious things said and objects hurled at them to arouse them from their sleep, when he rose within a moment, they were all up and moving. He felt like it was going to be a good group. Then it came to him—the lieutenant had appointed him platoon guide for the group the previous evening while they were having their orientation meeting. There would be a more formal meeting with the major and the entire faculty of the school today.

But first things first, get the men ready for PT. In less than ten minutes, the group was standing outside. He quickly organized them into the semblance of a formation. Taking his place at the front, he was hardly surprised when he saw the lieutenant coming toward them. The lieutenant was dressed for PT and took his place six paces in front of Foster. "Are the men formed for PT?" The lieutenant knew they were formed, but this was the military.

"Sir, the team is formed!" shot back Foster.

"PV2 Foster, in the future, you should give the order to fall in and then call the men to attention before turning the formation over to me or the NCO taking charge." The reprimand was given quickly and sharply. There was no animosity or hard edge, just the voice of instruction. Still, Foster was chastised, but he vowed not to make that silly mistake again. Abramson was certain that he wouldn't.

"At ease," Abramson instructed. He then proceeded to go into detail about what the next hour would contain for these men. Concluding, he asked, "Any questions?" They all knew enough to save their breath rather than waste it on foolish questions. "Attention" was the next command.

"First Sergeant, post" came the sharp command from the lieutenant.

Materializing from his position behind the little formation, the first sergeant came forward to a position halfway between Foster and the lieutenant. The lieutenant turned the formation over to the first sergeant and took his post behind them. No one had noticed that the entire six-man team commanded by Abramson had fallen in with the lieutenant.

The forty-something-year-old first sergeant was soon leading them in stretching exercises, and gradually, they worked through the entire muscular system. Then they executed a left face, were soon double timing, and ultimately route stepping at a pace they would not forget for a few days. The older man worked them for fifty minutes when they suddenly realized they were back at the barracks they had departed not so long ago. Leading them in stretching again, the top sergeant explained each exercise and its purpose to the group. Finally, he indicated that they could expect this every Monday morning throughout their training. "And I would encourage you to make it a part of your regimen for your military career." Calling Foster forward from the ranks, he turned the formation over to the trainee, with instructions to see to the personal hygiene of the troops and get them through the chow line. The next formation was scheduled in seventy-five minutes.

Falling into the barracks, the young men who had just finished what they considered a grueling basic training course were struggling for breath. As they headed for the showers, Wiznewski whispered, "That man never broke a sweat during that entire hour. I bet I lost five pounds keeping up with him."

Ash looked around and muttered, "I was watching that team, and they never took a deep breath. Those guys are remarkable, the condition they are in."

Nuckles said, "This is not going to be a piece of cake. As we started on that little jog, I noticed the other three teams were formed up on the other side of the office building. They went for a little jog. They didn't get back until we were breaking up. I believe these guys take this stuff seriously. We are going to get into the best shape of our lives. I thought I was in good shape." The two sport high school athletic star proclaimed. "But I'm dragging. If they keep running us like this, we'll either get tough or get gone, I imagine."

In a normal elite army training class, Nuckles's observation would probably have held true. In this case, however, there was never any doubt that all would finish. The only washouts would be if someone was physically injured and unable to complete the mission. This bit of information was, of course, withheld from the class. The bottom line was they had all recently completed basic and had achieved the picket fence on the profile line of their army physical they had been given upon induction into the force. The picket fence meant there were no significant physical restrictions on their activities. This was a requirement of all army advanced schools requiring extreme physical demands.

Even though two of them couldn't tell if shaving was necessary by looking in the mirror, they all had freshly shaved profiles when they emerged from the barracks twenty minutes later. In their freshly laundered fatigues, they cut a striking figure as they marched to the mess hall. Eating breakfast after PT had been found to significantly reduce the appetites of the men by the time honored tradition of trial and error, so they as all others in the military ate after exercise.

Stidham observing them from his office window thought, *They are the youngest group I have ever had. I hope their intelligence makes up for their lack of maturity.* As they marched by his window, his thoughts were interrupted by a call from Bringle. "I wanted you to know that we have a definite go for the mission. I will be out to work out the details of insertion and extraction later this week." He wasted no time in getting to the point.

Stidham could almost hear the clock ticking on the mission countdown. He had to get the entire team ready. He still didn't know how much time he had, but he knew it was definitely limited.

After filling their bellies, Foster formed the team up and marched them back to the barracks, thinking, *What do I do with them now?* He was finding the freedom of movement somewhat distracting after eight weeks of being marched by drill sergeants to every appointment, activity, or event he had needed to attend. For the group to be able to move at their own volition was invigorating.

Arriving back at the barracks, he was relieved to find that what to do next would not be a problem. Sergeant First Class DeWitt was waiting for them. He took them immediately in tow, explained that they would begin jump school that very day, and marched them away. Arriving at the jump school, they were taken into the pack shed by the instructor assigned to them, and their specialized training had begun.

The first thing they learned was that an airborne soldier never walked anywhere. The second thing was that even though they had spent two weeks training to become vehicle operators, they were not riding anywhere for this two-week period. As they began to learn the intricacies of packing their parachutes, they realized that this was important stuff. If you failed to pay attention, it was your neck on the line if the chute failed. None of them wanted that experience, so they paid close heed to the instructions. The instructor moved very quickly but he was extremely thorough in his presentation. He had never had a student incorrectly pack a chute, and he had no intention of letting one of these guys be his first.

Before they knew it, they had completed their first day. Coming back to the barracks, they were pretty much beat. They were not excited to find that there would be a school meeting for all faculty, staff, and students at 1900. They had to get to the mess hall, eat, and get back before the meeting. Once again, they were double-timing it not to impress anyone but to simply accomplish everything that had to be done.

At 1900, First Sergeant VunCanon was going down his roster. Seeing that everyone was present, he called them to attention. Within seconds, Stidham was coming into the large common area of the school facility. He instructed them to be at ease and take a seat. This was the first time he had had all of the staff present with the students. From this point on, he intended to do business this way. Even though technically, the trainees were separate from the cadre, he knew that they were all about to undertake an extremely dangerous mission. He had to begin building a single cohesive team.

First, he introduced the four team leaders. Then he mentioned the first sergeant. There was no need to introduce him as everyone already knew him and the role in which he functioned. At the mention of each name, he had them rise and tell the team something of their background. Then he continued through the balance of the cadre. Finishing with them, he turned to the trainees and introduced each of them. Instead of asking them to give their background information, he proceeded to tell some of their stories to the cadre. Wrapping up this phase of the meeting, he concluded, "As you can see, everyone here has unique qualifications to be on this team. For this mission to be successful, we all have to work as one. There may be times when you are asked to augment the personnel of another team, or you may be told to do something by one of the instructors, which seem contradictory of something you were told by another instructor. That can be frustrating. Remember, we may not all do every task exactly the same, but we do follow army doctrine in all that we do."

He paused to let his words sink in to his audience. Then he turned to the cadre, "Over the coming weeks, we will rotate primary responsibilities for training our recruits. I charge you to never forget that someone took you under their wing in the Nam and taught you what right looked like. Make this true for these men. At the same time, one team will be practicing our techniques for securing their portion of the village we will come to know as Duc Lo. Fire and maneuver teams will become closely coordinated by team leaders. We will work one team at a time. A second team will be tasked to provide OPFOR services at the Duc Lo facility. The fourth team will be preparing to provide primary training duties for the following week for our new members. Any questions so far?"

There were several. Taking them one at a time, he carefully laid out the plan. He had taken the recommendations for team activities and events that the team leaders had been tasked with preparing earlier, and now he presented them with a standard five-paragraph operations order for how the school would operate for the next six weeks. He was aware that his plan did not meet every contingency that might arise, but it was thorough as he could make it, and it would simply have to do. Having been given only partial information about his tasking, he could not presume to know all the factors that were mysteries to not only those who had given the tasks but also to those who would perform them as well.

Finally, Staff Sgt. Patrick Rhames spoke up. "Sir, we all figure we are here to perform some type of black arts op. What we don't seem to make any sense of is what these rookies are doing here with us. With all due respect, sir, this makes no sense."

There it was said and out in the open. Stidham had known that eventually he would have to answer this. "Staff Sergeant Rhames, your team has a mission. These men have a mission. While they are not the same, both are critical to the overall mission of team 7, Hotel Company, Second Ranger Battalion as assigned with additions and as augmented according to Special Order 70-436 from Department of the Army." He went on to explain that there would be plenty of operating room for everyone. He knew that Rhames was a very aggressive soldier who carried out his missions with gusto. Sometimes that gusto had approached the limits that could be tolerated, and more than once, it had been necessary for him to pull the good staff sergeant out of trouble. Still he was a dependable and smart operator who was fast on his feet and a quick thinker when placed in a crisis. Stidham was never sure if his actions were the result of conscious decisions or if they were simply reactions to circumstances where he found himself engaged. But he did know that, for all the dangers the man brought with him, he was an asset that they would need if they were to be successful.

Looking eye-to-eye at Rhames, he delivered his speech. Rhames never backed down, but he did recognize that he had to accept orders that he often did not understand or simply made no sense to him. The staff sergeant had long ago given up understanding the thinking that went on in the Ivory Towers, where all officers resided to his way of thinking. Stidham had given him a lot to chew on in his little speech. There was information there he had not had before, and before he reacted to the situation, he wanted to mull over what the major had said. If these new men were going into a combat zone with him, he wanted to make certain that they were ready to perform when they got there. He decided that they would get nothing but his best efforts to provide that readiness to them.

As for the new recruits to the operation, they were receiving news also. They had never considered that the older men would treat them as anything other than trainees. This aspect of jealousy or concerns about effectiveness had not occurred to them. They had heard talk of real-world missions, but that had translated to them differently than life-on-the-line missions they had just heard about. Suddenly, they were aware of a much more serious side of this training they had embarked on.

Woodie Foster looked at Nuckles and mumbled, "My old man used to tell me about his days in World War II, and he was always complaining about not knowing what was going on until he was smack in the middle of it. I think I might prefer not knowing to knowing, all things considered."

Nuckles thought for a moment and then replied, "Either way, I think I want to stay with the major. His way of leading is a lot better than what I saw in basic and a whole lot better than any leadership I was ever around on the outside. I like him, and I like these men who are working with us. I imagine to get us to where they have the confidence in us to do our jobs as well as we feel about those abilities. They will have to put us in some tight spots, but I appreciate that they will be there with us." At this point, he didn't know about the final stage of cross-country deployment they would be conducting. But Stidham, who had overheard the conversation from the back of the room, was feeling much better about his chances to pull this off. He had at least gotten through to one element of his team and felt good about the direction he was seeing that element go.

The next morning, it was the same routine for the trainees, with Foster taking the lead as platoon guide. The plan was for each man to serve one week as the platoon guide on a rotating basis. Foster had done a great job on day 1. He had succeeded in getting no serious demerits. In the view of the cadre team of First Lieutenant Abramson, this was a stellar accomplishment. How would day 2 go?

It didn't take long to find out. During the first mile of their daily three-mile run, Wiznewski went down. He felt something pop in his right knee, and suddenly, he could not bend his knee nor, for that matter, could he stretch it out to full extension. An ambulance was called for, and Wiznewski was soon on his way to the medical facility. Down to three students, the training continued as the instructors tried to get in as much training as they could during the limited time available to them.

After turning the team over to the jump school instructor, First Lieutenant Abramson went to the hospital to see about Wiznewski. He was greatly relieved when he was met in the hallway by Wiznewski walking normally. It seemed that the younger man had a torn cartilage in his knee. The cartilage had torn completely in two pieces. The end of one piece had originally flapped into the knee joint, causing the severe problem with the knee. After rest, ice, and manipulation, the piece had flapped back around it and was no longer a problem.

As the lieutenant went in to meet with the doctor who had examined Wiznewski, his mind raced. What did Wiznewski need from him, what was his ability to continue the training, what were the consequences if he did continue what they would do if he was unable to continue, and what impact would all this have on their mission? As these thoughts jockeyed for position in his brain, one very comforting thought came to him—it wouldn't matter in the long run. None of these were his decisions. He was playing with house money. All this would rest on the capable shoulders of Maj. William Stidham or someone further up the chain of command than him.

As he cleared these thoughts from his mind, he considered what the captain who had examined Wiznewski was telling him. There was a good possibility that he could continue the training with no further repercussions. If he did and there were to be additional problems, it was possible that he still would not need immediate surgery. Sometimes these injuries went on for years before they had to be resolved surgically. For now he was released back to full duty with no restrictions.

Abramson loaded him into his POV, a candy apple red Chevrolet Camaro, and started across post. Remembering the restrictions that the young PV2 had been subject to for the past two months, he offered to stop and get him something to eat at one of the restaurants on post. He was amazed and impressed by the answer. "No, sir, I'm behind on today's training already. I can't afford to miss anymore. If you would, sir, just take me to the jump school."

Abramson knew which of the trainees he wanted aligned to his squad if it came to choices. This young man had his head screwed on straight.

Foster was glad to see Wiznewski when he arrived back at the school. The jump school cadre had not been enthused about the story of Wiznewski. They had already written him off as a training casualty of the first week. With the rush to get this group through, they weren't surprised, but neither were they sympathetic. So it was with a grunt and a nod that Wiznewski was allowed back into the regimen.

Even given the lack of enthusiasm shown by the school personnel, Foster noticed that every time there was a short break in the regimen, Wiznewski was with one of the school leaders getting caught up on what he had missed earlier. This was the second big impression Wiznewski had scored for the team today. And they needed those points, tomorrow they would make their first tower jumps. During the afternoon session of the school, the team was introduced to the various aircraft used to deliver troops behind enemy lines for jumps into action. Nuckles was so intent on the instructor's explanation of jump procedures from the new C-141s that he didn't even notice the full colonel who had come to the training session until the group was called to attention by Sergeant First Class DeWitt, who was monitoring the team's activities for Stidham and Abramson.

"Carry on" was the quick reply of Col. David Dalembert, the assistant post commander. He would not ordinarily have been on such a mission as this, but when the BG in charge told him to send someone to an empty room, he decided that he would like to see some actual training getting done. So here he was. It seemed that PV2 Nuckles's mother, who had recently learned of his enlistment in the United States Army, had called to complain to her congressman about his enlisting without her knowledge. Would PV2 Nuckles please accompany him to post headquarters, where they would attempt to straighten out the mess?

As they drove back to post headquarters, the colonel listened as Nuckles told him the story. He had left home at seventeen, with his mom's knowledge but not her blessing. He had lived with his paternal grandparents until his graduation from high school. While living there, he had worked part-time and paid his grandmother rent. Also, his father had paid the grandmother a percentage of the child support he had agreed to pay the mother. No issues had ever been raised.

46

"Well, son, that's all well and good, but don't you think you should have turned eighteen before you joined the army?" quizzed the colonel.

"Yes, sir." The answer came back emphatically from the youngster. "I turned eighteen in January before I graduated high school. Sir, if you check with the school, you will find that they tried to make me bring a permission slip from a parent once for an absence. When they found I was an emancipated youth, they said it didn't matter. They never asked for anything like that again."

Upon arriving back at the post HQs, Col. Dalembert had gone in to meet with the garrison commander and explained the story to him. The garrison commander was glad to wash his hands of the matter and assigned the colonel to return the congressional staffer's phone call. After a short game of phone tag, they had talked, and the colonel had satisfied the congressman that the army was not kidnapping seventeen-year-olds off the streets of American cities or rural areas for that matter. After about an hour and a half, the colonel came into the waiting area to tell Nuckles he was free to return to his training. Forgetting that he had brought the youngster to HQs, the colonel never gave a thought to getting him back to his training area.

Nuckles had only been in the army a couple of months, but he had learned a few things. One was to never point out to a field grade officer any mistake he made. He simply saluted, did an about face, and went out the door. Arriving at the entrance to the facility and seeing no available transportation, he improvised. One hour and fifteen minutes later, he arrived back at the mock-ups of the air force planes used for jumping. Reporting to the NCOIC of the jump school, he resumed his place in the class. Again, Foster noted that the staff of the course was trying to catch Nuckles up at every opportunity for the balance of the day.

When they were released and sent back to their barracks at the end of the day's training, as usual, they were exhausted. As Foster thought back on how close he had come to losing two men under his command, he did not realize the impact those two soldiers had made for this group on those who had dealt with them that day. While losing these men would have been an administrative thing only, it certainly gave Foster insight into the intricacies of command. Not for many days would that come to pass.

And so the days of jump school went until they were ready for their first jump. Carefully preparing the chutes was their first chore of the day. Major Stidham had arranged that all their training jumps would be made from the new C-141s rather from the assorted aircraft used for jumping by the USAF. There was a reason for this, but the men did not yet know it, and the jump school NCOIC didn't question what the officer's had worked out as gentlemen's agreements. Further, all jumps would be rear ramp rather than door jumps. For such a small group, the cadre was puzzled but again provided the training requested without wandering out loud what was going on.

Stidham was busier than he had ever envisioned the life of a field grade officer in garrison possibly keeping him. He had his new company clerk setting up the orderly room and trying to get all the work done that had to accompany that. He had four of his NCOs out, giving road tests to his four new wheeled vehicle operators. This had been more of a challenge than he had thought since the person qualifying an operator on the DA Form 348 Military Driver's License must be qualified on that piece of equipment. Finding grunts (11B20 or higher) who were licensed had turned out to be a chore, but things had eventually worked out. Now all he had to do was document the road experience, and they would have qualified through OJT for their new MOS.

Meantime, he had to get them scheduled for the jump school. He had been able to get the four-week classes shortened to two because of the small number of candidates and because he was the proud former owner of a bottle of scotch, which now resided with the command sergeant major of the jump school. That wheel had been greased appropriately.

He had just come from the office of Ms. Vickie Cross, in whose good graces he now rested due to the dozen yellow roses, which had preceded him through her office door by the length of his arms. They had enjoyed catching up on the past few days, and Ms. Cross had seemed to come to the conclusion that maybe he hadn't caused her too much heartache after she had seen the roses. With a florist located just outside the gate to Clarksville, Tennessee, she would never understand why more soldiers were not able to get their record reviews done in a timely manner.

Additionally, he had four teams of his men working steadily on the logistical requirements for the new school. Just when they thought they had covered all the bases, someone would think of another issue, and off would go a detail to work on resolution. He was really proud of how the men had pitched in.

Probably, he thought Jamison and Mizell had put their minds and considerable expertise to maximum advantage and stepped the pace up for the whole team. Now Bringle was coming back for round 2 of whatever they were cooking up for his team. Since he didn't know exactly who "they" were, it was easy to imagine them in the greatest of uncomplimentary terms.

He was impressed that the teams were already developing their own personalities. The morning PT sessions were becoming quite competitive as each man and team strove to outdo the others. He knew that he had to hone that characteristic, as it was sometimes easy to let the competitive edge slip over the line and become a drawback to unit cohesion. Still he was pleased by the progress he observed, but he needed to keep himself aware of the pitfalls.

He saw Bringle pull his rental car into the visitor's space out in front of the office. As he came into the building, he heard PV2 David Cansler greet the civilian. "Sir, may I help you?" It was quite apparent that if he had business here, Cansler was going to take care of it. If not, he would shortly be hitting the road.

Good for Cansler. He's coming right along. The thought barely had time to form in Stidham's brain before there was a rap on the office door, and Cansler was inquiring, "Sir, are you expecting a Mr. Bringle?"

"Yes, PV2 Cansler, I am expecting him" was the courteous reply from Stidham.

"Sir, right this way, please," young Cansler announced as if there had been a chance the civilian would take off in a different direction. This brought a grin to the face of the major.

"Well, Bringle, what's the good news?" Stidham was upbeat as he looked over his visitor.

"I have received a go on our project. We have tracked the activity in our little compound, which is now being referred to as Duc Lo. We have access to the schedule of visitors to the site, which, to this point, has proven reliable, but we are still assessing the reliability of this source." Bringle quickly brought Stidham up to date on his progress. "Now how is the recruiting going here?"

Stidham nodded in acknowledgment of what he had just heard. "We actually got four volunteers from the list you developed on your last visit. They have finished their MOS qualification today and began jump school this week. They are living next door in the barracks. We are piecing together everything we need for the school. We have no resource restrictions. TRADOC (training and doctrine command) so far has not balked at anything we have requested. We are fat and sassy so far. We also picked up a young man for our company clerk from the list you developed."

"Great, I would like to meet them all while I'm here." Bringle offered this thought as Stidham walked around the desk. Bringle noticed the new format of the furniture as Stidham waved him to a seat.

"You met the company clerk," Stidham informed him. "The others are out on a mission right now. We'll get them in later."

Bringle then commented on the new furniture arrangement. Stidham was happy to change the topic. "First Lieutenant Abramson came up with this idea during the interviews. It seemed to have a great impact on our success." Stidham didn't think it any of Bringle's business as to the details of how the interviews had gone, so he offered no explanation.

"Good news." Bringle was glad to hear of the progress. Of course, with all the years he had known Stidham, it was, in no way, a surprise to him. "We have confirmed that there seems to be a regular pattern to the activity at Duc Lo. We are going to dub this operation as Operation Duc Lo 70. That should give the reporters a chuckle when this all comes out."

Stidham was somewhat concerned about the repeated references that Bringle made to the media. Being a professional soldier, he had never considered how the media would view his actions as the defining factor in what those actions would or should be. He had been taught that you recognized the right thing, and then you went and did it. Still, he supposed that the civilian had a different agenda than he, so they would naturally choose different options.

"What time frame do you think we can shoot for as far as operational readiness?" Bringle was ready to get to the meat of his visit. He needed a close estimate, so he could carry on his contacts with the North Vietnamese informant.

Stidham thought for a few seconds and then responded, "I don't guess you ever feel ready for one of these or that there is ever enough time for dry runs, dress rehearsals, etc. But I believe we could do this in about eight weeks. You know that we have yet to begin team operations other than to say we are running a school. Most of the men seem to know something else is coming, but they don't know any details."

"Well, maybe we can begin to fill in some of the blanks while I am here." Bringle obviously wanted to make a move.

"Let's discuss this over lunch. I would like Mizell, Jamison, Abramson, Scandretti, and VunCanon to join us at the O Club. (Officer's Club, even though technically VunCanon was not an officer, he could accompany the others as a guest. The civilian, as a senior government employee, was allowed in on his own merits.) Stidham picked up the phone, dialed VunCanon's extension, and requested that he arrange with the other four to meet them there.

"I would like to show you something on the way. We'll just meet them there." Stidham's statement was more of a directive. He had seized the momentum of the meeting. He was deciding where the meeting was being held, who was attending, and would have the prerogative of deciding when the crucial topics would unfold in the meeting. Bringle realized he would need his A game to play at this table. There was no room for error, or he would be simply window-dressing, which he had no intention of allowing.

As they drove to the Officer's Club, Bringle, who had spent some time at this post, realized they were not taking the shortest route. When he started seeing rifle range postings along the side of the road, he knew they had entered a tactical area. "See that range over there?" Stidham pointed to the newest sixteen-point record firing range. "We will be doing record fire there every Friday during the school—staff and trainees. All firing is computer scored, the latest and greatest."

"What about side arms?" Bringle had to get in some points or be overwhelmed.

"We will have no officer side arms as primary weapons. We will all demonstrate our mastery of the M16." Stidham's tone was adamant. "I want us all to be able to shoot and maneuver effectively," he added and then pointed to a range on the other side of the road. Even he had no idea of the profound effect this decision would have on the outcome of the team's mission. He would carry a sidearm as a secondary weapon eventually.

Marked by signage as an infiltration range, Bringle noticed the markings that this range was not in operational usage at this time. Questioning why the major would accept a below-standard training facility, he mused.

"It won't do you much good if it's not brought to ops," Bringle remarked.

"It is being refurbished as we speak." Stidham grinned like the proverbial possum eating briers. "You'll never guess who designed the refurbishment. We will be making frequent use of this facility. I am tight with the civilian in charge of range operations. I believe we can keep up the Keep Out signs for at least several weeks." Mentally, he noted that DeWitt and Goldman would need to make a class VI run that afternoon. He had to keep those skids greased.

Turning around in the POV (privately owned vehicle) was no issue, and in a few moments, they were driving into the lot at the Officer's Club.

Bringle thought as he reached for the door handle, "Ammo and pyrotechnics, are you having any problems there?" The meaning behind the question was "Have you even thought about these?"

Stidham sighed and replied, "We have activated an account at the issue point, and we have projected our usage for the year, broken down by quarters. Needless to say, we are projecting heavy usage in the next quarter but enough to avoid any questions through the end of the year."

"Good thinking." Bringle couldn't help but be impressed with the thoroughness of the operation that Stidham had initiated. Grudgingly, he admitted to himself that the ranger was probably better prepared for this task than he had originally thought. But then again, it never hurt to have someone looking over anybody's shoulder. Redundancy was the key when any glitch in a field operation could save lives, was a hard learned lesson, and was easily forgotten.

Stidham was accustomed to accounting for his thinking and his actions; he had never been one to hide behind his rank or his uniform. He knew that things had to be accounted for and that the sooner they were, the better the outcome of the accounting. He took none of the questions personally. He was at peace and willing to consider any reasonable suggestions. This was why he had been able to arrange for the use of the best range facilities with so little trouble. When he had gone to the range operations chief, he had gone hat in hand, so to speak. He had requested suggestions after detailing in broad terms the hoped for results. It seemed that not enough could be done to ensure the success of the operation.

Armed with this understanding, the two men moved to join the other five who waited for them in the bar of the Officer's Club. Moving quickly, they were able to just beat the lunch time rush of business. Stidham moved around the table verbally, introducing Bringle to the two lieutenants and reacquainting him with the others whom he had known or known of during his time in the secret war of Southeast Asia. Even though he had not worn the military uniform of his country, all knew that he had served with some degree of distinction. As such, he was regarded with esteem by these warriors.

As they enjoyed their meal, talk was limited. Finally when the waiter approached and wanted to know if they would like dessert, Stidham declined and told the group, "I don't know what you had planned for the afternoon, but I would like you to be in the common area at 1500. Top, could you make sure that we are set up for a top-secret briefing? If possible, bring your NCOICs of your teams. We have some very important things to cover."

At 1500, the common area had been transformed into a briefing room. The windows were covered, the area around the room secured, white noise played in the background on the ground floor. The briefing outline had been transformed to the butcher block with permanent markers. All the team leaders and NCOICs were assembled. It was a very somber group.

Bringle and Stidham walked into the area. Bringle removed the cover from the butcher block. There on the first sheet was the heading, "Operation Duc Lo 70"—the first these men had heard of the operation.

Stidham moved to the front of the room. "Men," he began, "we will be undertaking a serious mission. If we succeed, we will be able to bring back the first group of American POWs to be liberated during a war since World War II. We will be training for that eventuality over the next several weeks. Mr. Bringle and I have been putting the gloss on the operations plan for this undertaking. Each of you represents a major element in this plan. The school that we have set up here is also crucial to the success of this endeavor."

Flipping the chart, he began to explain the commander's concept of the mission. Four teams of rangers would go into North Vietnam in the area they had dubbed Duc Lo, secure the compound, photos included, relieve the guards of their security mission, evaluate the status of the POWs, prepare them for movement, execute the move to a nearby coastal area where they would transfer them into rubber inflatable lifeboats, and move them to a rendezvous point with a US Navy submarine. They would then be transported to Subic Bay in the Philippines, where they would become the talk of the nation. By the time anyone thought to ask, "How did you get out?" the team would have melted into the jungles from which they had come. Unspoken was the point that there would be a team presence on the submarine and at Subic Bay. As far as Stidham cared, Bringle could be there to manage the spotlight from that end.

He went on to task each team with developing a movement plan to move to the contact area. Captain (P) Mizell came over to Stidham and asked, "How do we get delivered?"

Stidham brusquely replied, "C-141, probably from Guam."

"I have been studying a new technique known as HALO. It might be the answer to getting in without being seen," Mizell explained the technique of high-altitude jump with extended free fall and then preset pressurized capsulated opening devices for the parachutes.

Stidham was somewhat skeptical at first of this idea. "I guess we would still make fine targets at those lower altitudes," he objected.

"Not if we jumped at night in black suits." Mizell was warming to the task. He had been to the jump school at Ft. Bragg, where the Eighty Second was desperately developing new ideas for remaining relevant to the developing techniques of warfare. After all, they did not wish to become redundant at this time when cutbacks would surely be coming at the end of the war.

Stidham thought about this. "Let's make some of these jumps part of the school curriculum, get the entire team some technique improvements, and evaluate the skill sets required." Mizell had a feeling that they would be using the new idea.

Stidham was impressed with the young captain, soon-to-be major. He had found that the captain's promotion date was set for March 26, so he felt comfortable that he would have the younger man with him for this mission before promotion stole him away.

Next, he called First Lieutenant Scandretti and Sergeant First Class Taylor over to his area. He described the infiltration range he had made arrangements to have dedicated to his team for the next few months. Picking up one of the photos of Duc Lo, he commented, "I wish I knew an enterprising young officer and NCOIC who could make something very much like this appear on that range." Stidham looked at them expectantly.

Scandretti could not resist a challenge. "Sarge, don't you think we could do that?"

Taylor was nodding. "Yes, sir, I believe we could. But, sir, if time is of the essence, that will take probably three days for our team to build, assuming, of course, that we can get the materials. There is a mock-up Vietnamese village here on post that has been used for some time to acclimate deploying troops going over there. We might be able to use it."

"There are a couple of reasons I wanted to avoid the mock-up," Stidham quickly answered. "This is the actual objective we will be dealing with, not a reasonable facsimile, and second, we would have its exclusive use, not having to schedule our time. For that matter, if we felt we needed additional iterations of some phase of the operation, we would have no encumbrances."

"We'll get started with the plans right now. May we work with this while we're in here?" Scandretti knew that he couldn't take the classified material from the room, but he needed to study the setup to attempt to replicate the structures and the area surrounding them.

"Certainly, use it as long as you like in here." Stidham was assured that he would have a new playground for his troops to train. If he was correct in his judgment, it would not take them three days. They had embellished the time requirements just in case they ran into unforeseen obstacles. Stidham laughed to himself. Only in the army would you find a civil engineer in the infantry, and then the thought occurred to him to be thankful for such a system. Where would he be if not for the talents of these men?

As he looked around the room, it struck Stidham how cohesively this group was coming together to put this plan into reality. Already, he could see the team building taking effect. Approaching VunCanon, he observed, "Top, these men are really digging in." VunCanon couldn't have been prouder if he had been at his first Little League practice with his firstborn child.

Bringle, who was accustomed to one-man shows and limited engagements, looked at the same scene and saw chaos. He was growing apprehensive of anything organized coming from so many people going off in so many different directions. He could not see the head of the animal leading all the parts back into an organized entity.

At about this point, Stidham headed for him. "How do you feel about the timing for the mission?"

"Well, I heard what your captain was saying about night ops, and I have to say that sounds intriguing." Bringle was not going to be put on the spot about this aspect of the plan. Stidham nodded and said, "I guess I wasn't specific enough. I meant the overall timing."

Bringle realized his misunderstanding of the question. Shrugging, he said, "Until we have more historical data, it will be hard to say. We believe there will be ongoing traffic through this station. We are asking NSA to consult back files for any photos or any other intelligence regarding these grid coordinates. So far, they have not found any records of this place popping up on anybody's radar. We think it may be relatively new."

This news caused a mixed reaction from Stidham. He was glad to know that there appeared to be a good chance that further usage of the compound was expected by the North Vietnamese. However, it was cautionary that other agencies were being involved. He remembered his grandmother telling him more than once when he was a child, "Too many cooks spoil the soup." He hoped that he was just being paranoid. Still, it was troubling to his way of thinking.

Stidham once again caught the attention of VunCanon, "Top, if you could, kind of ride herd on this for the next few days. Keep the guys going at it, and please give them the encouragement to develop plans from outside the box. Of course, we have to observe operational security (OPSEC) measures in all phases of our plan development. Let's get them together on Friday and get a reading on what the progress has been."

"Right, sir, I'll be after them hard," the first shirt replied. He had his first tasking outside the normal duties of the top enlisted man in the operation. He felt totally energized.

At 1700, there was a bit of commotion next door as the trainees were returning from their daily excursion. They had completed their second day of jump school that day and were now more than wheeled vehicle operators. They knew the rigors of jump school would ramp up the next day. Stidham had promised Bringle the chance to meet them, so he excused himself and the civilian from the ongoing discussions in the common area and took him next door.

As they entered the door, Foster spotted them first and, leaping to attention, shouted, "Attention! Lead the way, sir." Stidham put the group at ease. He gathered them around the front of the barracks in what had come to be their day room. "I want you guys to meet Marty Bringle. He is a government employee, and in some ways, he played an important role in your being selected for attendance in this course. He may want to talk to you as a group, or perhaps he would like to speak to you individually." Stidham had thus left it up to Bringle as to how he would handle this interplay with these young men.

Bringle was once again struck by how these young soldiers had already begun to bond with the major who was probably as old as most of their fathers. He thought this man is a born leader. He doesn't even realize how dynamic he is, and these guys already would do anything for him. "Guys, as you know, there is a hands-on, real-life component to this training you have undertaken. We are appreciative of your willingness to undergo the rigors of the training and of this first mission you will seek to carry out. These missions are potentially dangerous, but they carry a very real chance of making a real difference in the war effort. If we are successful in our actions, you may become the Sergeant York or the Audie Murphy of this war." Bringle meant to be encouraging, but he had slipped over the line and become maudlin. He had lost his audience. While they remained polite, they had heard all of the hero talk they could stand. Stidham had a sinking feeling that the subject of barracks talk that night had been decided.

Stidham hoped that Ash would not give him the treatment he had during the interview process. While he understood the frustration of the young troop, he did not need the team to make an enemy of Bringle. He had his priorities in order from that perspective. He decided it was time to wrap this session up.

"Mr. Bringle has had a long couple of days. I imagine the jet lag is beginning to catch up to him." Stidham extended a way out to the civilian. "Will you be able to stay over until tomorrow?" He really did not know what the plans were for the agency man.

"I have to catch a flight this evening back to Washington." Bringle's reply was really a release for the major. He never felt entirely comfortable when Bringle was around. He always felt that the man was putting on a show to a certain extent. This was not who Stidham was nor did he aspire to be. For that matter, he couldn't think of any of friends who shared this trait. He understood that they would be acquaintances and associates but never friends. He could live with that.

Bringle had left the meeting with the new trainees. In his mind, the meeting had gone extremely well. He was impressed with the newest members of the ranger team. They were still in the dark about the details of the mission. But only slightly more so than the more experienced leaders of the team. They didn't have the need to know everything. This thought made him feel better about the plan that was beginning to come together.

His contact with the leaders, while not acrimonious, had not been thoroughly enjoyable. These men had all had some contact with him in the field except for the one young lieutenant whose single tour had brought him into Nam after Bringle's departure. Still, he felt there was a working relationship there that could be developed over time.

Week 2

Dallas 28–New York Giants 10
Baltimore 24–Kansas City 44

PV2 Ash had been selected as platoon guide for this week of the school. Foster had thought he would be glad to give up the placard to him, but when the time came, he was actually wistful for the arm placard. He had come to enjoy the role and was appreciating the role of leadership more every day. However, he knew that each man had been selected because of leadership traits he had exhibited and deserved a chance to prove a leader lurked inside of him as much as any other.

As the men finished their packing chores, they placed the chutes on their backs, slung the emergency chutes on, and moved out smartly from the packing shed into the green ramp area. Here they were briefed about today's mission, given the weather report for the area, and wished godspeed by the briefer for the day. Shortly they were notified that the C-141 was at the terminal, and loading would begin in five minutes. They suddenly all noticed that it was time for a latrine break. Reassembling after this task was taken care of, they shuffled out to the temporary stairs leading to the front door of the airplane.

As they entered, they were checked off by the crew master. He then turned them over to the jumpmaster, who checked their equipment, assigned them seats, and checked the details of the weather forecast. He was pleased everyone had their equipment, and the weather was cooperating. Giving the all clear to the crew master, he took his seat and awaited takeoff.

As the plane took off and drew up to its cruising altitude, Foster was musing over how they had gotten to this point. He had been challenged to make the right decisions, keeping the detachment in a cohesive state. Now as they approached the drop zone, the jumpmaster indicated that it was time to prepare for the jump. Each man stood up, hooked his parachute static line into the overhead slide, and moved nearer the rear ramp of the plane.

When the green light came on, the ramp was lowered, and the jumpmaster made his forty-six points of contact with each man, making sure that every snap and buckle was correctly positioned. As the ramp reached its optimum position, Foster walked to the edge. Feeling a twinge of reluctance at the last second, he looked back at the jumpmaster for the thumbs-up signal. He never saw it. The momentum of his movement down the ramp kept him coming right off the ramp. The next thing he knew, he was airborne.

What a feeling he was experiencing. He had never felt anything like this in any of his previous activities. He suddenly knew what he had been born to do. After a few short seconds, he felt the snap of the static line yanking the chute from its pack and deploying into the brilliant sunshine. Behind him came Knuckles,

Wiznewski, and Ash. They each in turn walked the ramp, turned as they had seen Foster do, and were snatched from the ramp and into the freedom of flight. Each man knew the feeling that he was feeling was unique to him—no one else had ever felt this way. Only later would they realize that this feeling was close to universal among those who had gotten this far in their training, but for now, they simply enjoyed the sensation of flying through the air.

In a few short seconds, it seemed the ground was rushing toward them, and it was time to prepare for landing. They had been dropped into the largest drop zone on Ft. Campbell, and the area was wide open. Fortunately, they would not have to deal with overgrown vegetation in their landing area. Hitting the ground, they were in a flexed position so that their entire body could absorb the impact of the landing. They quickly went into a roll and began to gather their chutes for storage.

Ash quickly took inventory of each man to be sure that there were no injuries. Finding none, he organized them to move on off to the edge of the wooded area bordering the drop zone. It seemed to be nearby, only later did they realize that it was over a mile away. They were moving across the drop zone with no thought of noise discipline, unit integrity, or reconnoitering the area when they came upon the jump school instructor who had been placed there to make sure they were all right.

Unknown to the little detachment, there had been an emergency vehicle parked in the area in case the results of the drop had not been as great as they had achieved. The cadre sergeant handed Ash the packet he had been given and watched as Ash stood down the team and opened the packet. Inside were a compass and a map of the area. In block letters across the top of the map was written, "Good luck on getting back." It was about the time that Ash read this when they heard the sound of an engine being started and realized that the cadre sergeant had left them. The final phase of the jump was to get back to the school. From the limited map reading skills he had been taught in BCT, Ash figured it was about eight miles back to the school. But he had a map and a compass and plenty of good company. They headed back to the school.

After approximately four miles at a good pace, they were pleased to see the sergeant waiting for them beside the road. "I thought you guys might get hungry, so I ordered a gourmet lunch for each of you." He grinned widely at his witticism and handed over four boxes of C rations, which they, of course, had to sign a head-count sheet to validate their receipt.

The C rations, while not the best food ever consumed by humans, were filling, and soon the detachment was ready to move out. With only a little grousing about the trek, while the good sergeant was riding in his quarter-ton chariot, they headed down the road.

"I wonder why they trained us to drive those things. I guess they wanted us to know how comfortable they rode while we were marching everywhere."

Wiznewski was not really upset, but in the time, honored tradition of the military felt obligated to complain about something.

Nuckles looked down the road where the quarter ton had recently disappeared and mused, "My daddy would call this riding on shank's mare. Well, I can tell you shank is getting tired, but we will be OK. Did any of you feel the exhilaration when we jumped while ago?" This got them back on track. They were soon comparing the feeling of coming down, feeling the chutes yank them back to their surroundings, and then the feeling of seeing the earth coming at them at an alarming speed. They all agreed it was exactly what Nuckles had labeled it—exhilarating.

With no sign of weariness, they were soon at the pack shed. Their instructions had been to land navigate to this structure, and they had covered the distance to the pack shed quickly. Upon arriving, they were instructed to come into the shed, inspect their chutes for any damages incurred in the day's activities, and begin to repack for the coming jump tomorrow.

That evening, they had a small celebration at the Enlisted Club on post. None of them had their POVs at the post. They did splurge and share a taxi to the club and for the return trip. Before they were aware of it, the dawn was breaking, and they were on their way to PT, even though they had found they would be getting plenty of exercise today.

Two weeks after his first trip, as the negotiators were leaving for Paris, Bringle was first in line in the private flight terminal at Dulles International Airport. He was revved up for this trip. He was unable to sleep on the flight across the Atlantic, even in the reclining seats of the government jet they were taking. It seemed to him that they were forever in getting to the first negotiating session of this round. It was a tremendous relief to him when he spotted Cho Dinh in the North Vietnamese team as they arrived. It seemed the day would never end.

That evening, he returned to the French restaurant where he had been approached by the North Vietnamese agent on the last trip. After dawdling over his food for two hours, he realized that there would be no contact that evening. Disappointed, he returned to the legation headquarters. As he filled out the form to send the encrypted message to the ADO, he was feeling greatly depressed.

The next morning, he was having breakfast continental style in the hotel restaurant when he noticed a disturbance in the lobby. Rising out of curiosity to get a better view, he moved a few steps from his table. When he sat back down, he noticed a scrap of paper had appeared on the table. *Amazing*, he thought, *I was never more than four feet away. I am trained to be observant, and yet twice he has left me notes that I didn't notice.* Opening the note, he read, "Check? 100,000 for schedule."

He was convinced of the author's meaning. He was somewhat frustrated at not being able to drive the train as far as timing the meetings and the drops, but he was ecstatic that the contact had been reestablished. He hurried back to the eleventh floor of the hotel to the security of the headquarters of the peace mission and drafted another message to the ADO, this time relaying the news of the most recent contact. In Foggy Bottom, it arrived in the dead of night. The watch officer decided it would save until morning.

Halfway through the morning session, he was jolted out of his mind game by the realization that he had been called on in the text of the meeting, and the participants were waiting for his response. How embarrassing; he didn't have a clue what he had been asked. "Perhaps we should make this a sidebar issue." He finally managed to get out and was genuinely surprised when the chief North Vietnamese negotiator smiled his way and, through his interpreter, answered, "Precisely how I would have proposed this be handled."

He didn't have time to see the look of concern pass between the Austrian and the head of security for the American team as he and Dinh rose to go to the room where side issues were relegated. He quickly discerned that the issue had been how to incorporate the production of the agrarian North into the more domesticated and industrialized South after the cease-fire took place. When Bringle arrived in the sidebar room, he was handed a sheath of papers by Dinh. Quickly, the Vietnamese pointed out several items that would have to be acted upon, either in their current form or in amended versions.

He once again was impressed that the man from the North had maneuvered him into this seemingly innocuous meeting. As he was coming to appreciate this, he also realized that the continuation of these minor points would provide cover and concealment for their further meetings if they were to happen. He had a strong suspicion that those meetings would be happening. During the midday break, he returned to the hotel.

Arriving on the eleventh floor, he was abruptly stopped by the communications guru for the mission. "Sir, this came for you. We just now got it decrypted." Thrusting a clipboard at Bringle, he waited for him to sign for receipt of the communication. Bringle scrawled his name close to the required place and was off to his room. Only in the confines of his room did he read the message. "Proceed as needed."

He had been given the green light to go at his discretion. He immediately picked some plain writing paper from his briefcase and prepared a note to his newfound friend. "What route would you take to Geneva?" He then went over the unimportant changes to the documents. He had been called upon to inspect, carried them to the chief of agriculture for his approval, and, having received it, slipped his note into the stack of papers.

He was ready for the afternoon bargaining session. After about an hour, Mr. Dinh respectfully inquired if the American had been able to affect the amendments they had discussed at the previous meeting. The American, Bringle, replied that he had some counter proposals, and they retired to the sidebar room they had used earlier. Bringle was becoming comfortable in that room. Handing over the documents, he indicated the changes that had been made. Mr. Dinh indicated that he would have to get the approval of the head of mission for the industrial section. They never mentioned the other pressing matter they were resolving.

The two men returned to the bargaining session, which seemed to go on forever. Points that were best described as the ultimate in minutiae to those not intimately involved were taking hours to even be defined. No wonder progress was so slow. When Bringle returned to the hotel, he was again met by the communications man. "Sir, some more information came over from the Department of Agriculture for you this afternoon." Once again going through the validation procedure, Bringle retrieved his information. This time, upon examining it, he wanted to turn a cartwheel. There in the grainy image transmitted through the underwater trans-Atlantic cable was the compound he had nicknamed by now as Duc Lo, deserted, no guards, and no sign of any Americans. The attached analysis statement indicated no human activity in the compound for twenty-four hours.

Bringle noted this was day 4 of the flyovers since the PWs had first appeared. He wondered if this was a typical length of stay there for a group. He made a note to himself to check on this in the future. Since this round of the diplomatic mission would be wrapping up tomorrow, he knew he was not going to get a chance to run this by Cho Dinh in the near future.

The next day, Dinh indicated that he had an approved copy of the negotiated transcript they had been working on for the past two days. As they entered the sidebar room to exchange documents, Bringle noted an extra sheet of paper stuck to the back inside cover of the document protector as he received it. By the time he had returned to his seat, the sheet of paper was safely tucked into his inside jacket pocket.

Arriving back at the eleventh floor of the hotel, Bringle pulled the sheet out of the pocket. Neatly printed was the following: Route to Geneva; Take Autobahn 437 to Exit 113, that will be federal Highway 36, go to 38th St., turn right, go to 45th Ave., you are looking for 1429 on the right. Accounting for shopping while there; Use grocery at 1827 38th St., laundry at 3793 18th Ave. They will take care of all your needs for cleaning." He now knew how to pay his informant. He still needed something tangible to send any funds that way, but he understood the routing process he was to use.

When the mission wrapped up, Bringle skipped the photo ops at the conclusion. While the diplomats were always ready for pictures, he had learned never to willingly give up his likeness to anyone. He was already lumbering toward Charles de Gaulle Airport and the jet that waited to take them back to the United States. He had lots of work to do.

Landing briefly at Dulles, he transferred to a commercial flight going into Nashville, Tennessee. He arrived there just as the sun was peeking over the horizon. Grabbing his bags, he hurried to the car rental counter and was soon on his way out of the airport. One hour later, he was sitting at the main gate of Ft. Campbell, Kentucky. He was soon checked into the guest quarters on post. He sat down and made a few notes on his legal pad before heading over to Campbell Field to find Stidham and his ranger school.

Meanwhile, back at Ft. Campbell, the race to make rangers from raw recruits was progressing at its full-throttle pace. While not seeming to hurry, there was never a slow moment as these young men were under constant supervision and being presented training opportunities.

Heading to the pack shed, they inspected their chutes, strapped them on, and moved to the green ramp. Once again loading into the cavernous C-141, they were struck by how much room there was for them to move around. The room was soon filled as those on orders for jumping that day were called, and the on-call jumpers were loaded aboard. These were men who needed to keep their jump status current but whose jobs frequently prevented them from jumping as a unit. The plane was quickly filled, and once again, they were airborne. The trip to the drop zone was not as quick as the previous day's drop had been, and looking at his notes, Ash realized why they were jumping into a slightly more remote DZ than yesterday. He was somewhat concerned when he realized his oversight, thinking, *What else have I overlooked? Oh well, it's too late to worry over spilled milk now.*

Once again, the jumpmaster moved them to their stations, and they stood up, hooked up, and shuffled to the ramp to paraphrase the old marching song they had heard ever since beginning CBT. This refrain was taking on new meaning to them now. Today's jump order had been rearranged, and Nuckles led off, followed by Wiznewski, Foster, and Ash. They would make sure that as platoon guide of the week, the man in charge, was last to leave the plane in case there were any issues with any jumpers. As with the previous day, there were none.

Once again, they were soon snapped back to reality from the near euphoria they had experienced immediately after leaving the plane by the snap of the static line breaking the chutes from the canvas containers, which they were stored inside. As they came back to reality and looked around them, it suddenly dawned on them how much smaller the DZ for this exercise was than the one for the previous day. They began to do some slip-screening to achieve a better landing angle, and soon they were on the ground and securing the area.

During the debriefing of the prior day's mission, there had been several things pointed out to them that they had failed to perform upon landing and during their move back to the origin of the mission. Ash intended to see that those things were not repeated today. Upon reaching the tree line, which had been only about eight hundred yards away from their landing today, they found their friend from the school cadre waiting for them again. Once again, he handed over the packet labeled "Jump Team Leader." Inside were the same items as yesterday. Today he also handed them the obligatory C rations they had received at the halfway mark yesterday.

Ash looked at him and said, "Giving those out early today, Sarge?"

"Well, you guys showed yesterday that you could read a map and follow the terrain back. I thought I'd give you a little independence today. Maybe not tell you when you're hungry." With that, he swung into his quarter-ton general purpose (GP) vehicle known by millions as a Jeep and was gone.

Ash looked at the map, and it was soon apparent that they had indeed been given some lengthening of the leash they were accustomed to having constrain them. If they went by the closest road route, it would be over ten miles. By going cross-country that distance could be cut to about seven miles. It looked like they would have to skirt around the edge of a small lake. His fledgling knowledge of reading topographical maps told him there was more to this than just going near the lake.

He was faced with a conundrum. If they took the longer route, it would be obvious they were afraid to take chances. If they took the shorter route with the inherent risks and maybe some with which he wasn't familiar, they might be letting themselves in for an even more difficult crossing. Then a stroke of genius occurred to him. He had heard rumors from the other companies in his BCT Battalion that Nuckles had really been a shining star at map reading and interpretation of the symbols contained on the topographical maps used by the military.

Calling Nuckles over, he very quickly addressed the problem. Nuckles was bewildered at first. This was the first time since he had raised his right hand for the oath that anyone had asked his opinion of anything. He paused for a moment, and then he ventured his opinion. "If we go the way you have laid out here, we are going to be heading through a very heavily marshy area right through here. I would be very concerned about this area right now after the heavy thunderstorms we have had for the past week." His finger pointed out a few plant-looking diagrams on the map.

"The map shows a trail going through here, but again, look at these elevation lines. There is a hundred-foot bluff located right in here." Once again, he was pointing to the tightly drawn contour lines indicating steep terrain. However"—he continued to study the map—"if we took the road for the first two miles and then took this trail through here, we still save about a mile and a half. That might be our best option."

There he had given the man in charge his opinion without forming it into a recommended course of action, but he had couched his language in such a way that there was no doubt which action he would take if the decision were left to him. He closely watched Ash's face. This was a new experience for both men, collaborating as it were on an important decision. Nuckles was anxious to assure himself that he had not offended the other man with his forthrightness, but he was aware of the power of the suggestion he had made. Ash, on the other hand, now needed to sell his course of action as his plan to maintain his leadership of the detachment.

The other two members of the detachment watched with interest as the two men discussed the solution to the problem. Finally, Foster broke the silence. "I think this is part of the play. I think they have been giving us opportunities to brainstorm the problems we have had, but we have been seeing them as problems for the leader. If I get a vote on this, I vote that we follow Nuckles's path. That is the most commonsense approach to me." He thought about his outburst and then fell silent.

Wiznewski added, "Ash, if you don't want to go along with Nuckles's recommendation, we will back you whichever plan you decide to follow because you are the appointed leader of our group." Nods from the trio emphasized that there were no superegos to be dealt with on this matter. They were unanimous in their support for Ash as the team leader.

After hiking about two miles down the road, they cut through on the path recommended by Nuckles. The sergeant from the jump school who had driven a very short distance before stopping to observe which option they would follow saw them start down the road and went on his way, confident that they had adopted the longer route due to their reluctance to take a chance. He was not there when they made the turn onto the trail. When he reported back to his superiors, they had listened and estimated the time the detachment should be coming into the pack shed. They had released all the staff to be back at 1730, a half hour before the detachment would arrive according to their calculations.

When the NCOIC drove up to the shed at 1715, he was startled to see the detachment sitting on the benches around the outside of the pack shed. "Well, you guys made good time. How long have you been here?" his query was kind of blasé.

"We've been here about forty-five minutes, Sergeant First Class," replied Ash.

They were brought into the pack shed pronto. They immediately commenced their inspection/repack activities to prepare for the next day. While they were tending to their business, the NCOIC got down to his business with the watcher/observer he had sent to the drop zone. He asked for a detailed report of what had happened in the DZ. After hearing the report of the staff sergeant he had sent to observe the detachment, he was impressed that they had finally discovered cooperation as a tactic for survival, but he was still mystified about how they had shaved so much time off the march without taking the riskier option. They had some new material for their daily after-action report.

The detachment had moved on to preparing for the coming day's jump. They were ready for the AAR (after-action review) when they were summoned into the facility meeting room.

The facility NCOIC decided to personally conduct the AAR rather than turning it over to a subordinate. His interest had been piqued by the events of the day. He started the meeting by reviewing the load out for the flight, which had been rather uneventful, and then covered the jumpmaster's report of the flight, again indicating a clean operation. He congratulated them on getting all personnel out in good time while still over the DZ's landing window. His coverage of the landing itself was rather perfunctory until he came to the part of preparing to move to the rally point (RP), which was the pack shed.

At this point, he began to quiz Ash about how he made the decision concerning the route. Somewhat sheepishly, Ash told him of his involvement of Nuckles in the map interpretation, but he stressed that he had made the decision ultimately, hoping to steer what he was increasingly concerned was going to be a tongue-lashing for the team away from Nuckles and to take the blame, if there was any. He was amazed when the NCOIC walked over to Nuckles and himself and said, "You guys are finally getting it. God gave each of you brains. Use them. Work together. Today we gave you time to work this detail out because we gave you more time yesterday, and you didn't take advantage of it. When the situation allows for more than a reaction, gather all the information you can get your hands on so you can make the best decision. Don't just take what is given and not develop it unless in the heat of the moment that is called for."

He paused to look around the room. He noticed Ash and Foster intently studying their boots. He decided it was time to pick them up a little. "While it took you a good time to get this concept, I have to tell you that most of the teams that come through here never get this. So you get an attaboy for that." He then went to how they made such good time on the march from the DZ to the pack shed. He didn't exactly mention the abundance of egg on the faces of the facility cadre over that quick arrival, but he did mention that they had been observed moving on the range road at a pace that should have resulted in a much later arrival. He was curious as to how that arrival had been enhanced. He was really expecting to get a confession that they had gotten a lift from one of the cattle cars used to transport troops around the ranges who weren't expected to be as motivated as this group. He was astonished when Ash gave him his answer.

"Well, you see, Sergeant First Class, once again, PV2 Nuckles spotted a firebreak that cut across the area, and we took that way as a shortcut. Since we were given the map and the compass, we thought it would be all right." His voice trailed off as he gave the explanation.

"Aha!" exclaimed the NCOIC. "We know about that firebreak, but it does not go anywhere near all the way through to this area." He still thought he was going to nail them for getting a lift and was growing weary of what he thought was a failure to cooperate and own up to what they had done.

Again, he was floored when Nuckles bashfully said, "Well, you see, Sergeant First Class, we had a little celebration last night at the EM club. I happened to hear some of the engineer boys from the National Guard (NG) unit that is reworking the firebreaks on this side of post this week, telling about what they had just finished. I happened to remember the number of the one they had just finished and where they said it came out now. This was the most current information we had, so we used it. The way that firebreak runs now gave us the chance to shave off about a mile and a half from our march. You might say we found a shortcut for our ten-mile march." By the time he finished, he was completely red-faced. He suspected that he was going to be in big trouble. It was his turn to be amazed when the first-class sergeant walked over and proclaimed him "hero of the battle." With this designation, he was cognizant that he was not in any trouble for his outburst, but rather it was expected that he would take an action as long as he could rationally defend the execution of that action.

They quickly went over the operation for the next day's jump. This time, Ash was ready with questions about the DZ they would be using and seeking more details about the post landing operation they would be expected to execute. The NCOIC was suitably impressed that the team was coming along with the tactical understanding of the jumper's mission as well as the physical ability to make the jumps.

Stidham had unobtrusively slipped in to the area. He was unseen but not unhearing as the scene in the conference room unfolded. He was not only impressed with the problem-solving skills the detachment had shown but also with the esprit de corps that he sensed was developing with rapidity on the detachment. He was grateful that in a few days, jump school would be complete, and his team would take over responsibility for the total training package.

As the team headed for the barracks, he fell into place in the formation and ran with them. When the men realized he had joined them, they were eager to express their exuberance over the AAR. They quickly related the whole story to him, which came across rather disjointed since it was delivered on the run, by four men not planning to take turns telling the story. Oh well, they had been rewarded with a major attaboy for their efforts.

As the team fell out of the formation, they headed for the barracks. Someone said they should have a celebration tonight for the good job we did today. Ash replied, "My celebrating will have to wait. I'm going to spend some time going over tomorrow's mission, and then I'm putting my mama's little boy to bed. Nuckles, would you sit with me for a few minutes?"

He wanted to go over the area where they would be operating tomorrow, and he wanted the benefit of Nuckles's uncanny ability to interpret the map. He also wanted to pick up as much of that ability as he could get into his skull. He suspected that in days to come, this would become an urgent issue. Nuckles was happy to spend time sitting on a bunk going over the details of their DZ.

After about thirty minutes, he looked over at Ash and wondered, "Do you suppose this is all a red herring?"

Ash perplexed, looked up, and said, "How do you mean?"

"Well, they have not given us any information about the next day until today. Admittedly, we never asked for it until today. They seem glad that we asked, but what if there are other things they are looking for from us? What if this is all designed to draw us further down the line, to get us to dig for something else, or, who knows, react to false information? It just seems to me we are trusting blindly in what we are being told. Maybe we should be skeptical. Remember how the NCOIC was about our story about the route? Now I admit that he said he didn't know about the rerouting of the firebreak, but maybe they have something else planned for us."

Ash was more than a little discomfited by this part of their conversation. "Are you saying that we shouldn't plan for this mission based on the information we have been given?"

"No, what I am saying is that we shouldn't go in there tomorrow, thinking that we have this thing figured out. We should look for holes in the story. I don't know what the details are, but I have a feeling that they are going to throw us a curveball at some point of this." Nuckles sat pensively for a second and then added, "I guess what I'm saying is to make the best plan we can but don't marry ourselves to the plan. I think they will do something to force us to alter or even abandon the plan."

Ash nodded. "I see what you mean. Thanks for the help with the map. It seems that each drop, we get a smaller and smaller target. I guess they think we are getting better at controlling our descent. See you in the morning." With that, he began to fold the map and put away the notes he had prepared from the afternoon briefing. He was troubled by Nuckles's assessment that there would be an unforeseen variant thrown into the play tomorrow, but right now he couldn't figure out what it would be. He would have to react to it tomorrow.

The next day dawned sunny and bright. There were just a few fluffy clouds to be seen as they finished their morning PT session and moved in to their personal hygiene and breakfast period. Woodie Foster slipped up to Nuckles and said, "I saw you and Ash going over some pretty good stuff last night. All last week, I kept feeling like I was reacting to crises not really preparing for action. I think now that I was trying to do way too much and not using you guys to help me."

Nuckles smiled and said, "Last week was a different animal. We were in a whole different environment. If you had tried to involve us in every decision, nothing would have gotten done. You did fine." He added the last thought reassuringly, making certain that the young man did not think he was being critical of him. "As a matter of fact, you did much better than any PG we had in basic where I was."

"Still, I felt like I learned a lot yesterday from the way Ash handled the entire operation. He showed me how to get input from the team without losing control of the mission. I was so scared of losing control that I couldn't let you guys help where it was needed. I'll do better next time." Foster was obviously learning from the situations he saw his peer having to deal with in this role. Nuckles felt that he would do better. These highly motivated smart guys were beginning to feed off one another, and the team was sure to grow. Their capabilities were definitely on the upswing.

As they took the trail over to the jump school at an easy pace, Wiznewski laughed out loud. "I was thinking that we don't have a real good grip on this thing yet. These old boys cook something new up for us every morning. The smarter we think we are, the dumber we must seem to them. Experience sure is a good teacher."

By now they were coming into the pack shed, and the banter was knocked off. The serious business of jumping out of airplanes had now absorbed their attention for another day. They quickly performed their checks of the chutes they had prepared the previous afternoon and were soon moving to the green ramp area. Once again, the C-141 filled with other soldiers needing to make their jumps.

As they took off from the runway, each man was alone with his thoughts for a brief time. Wiznewski thought something felt different and mentioned it to Ash, who was behind him in the jump order that day. Since there were no windows in the cargo compartment where they were located, he couldn't tell that they were following a different flight path than they had on the first two jumps. Just as they had expected, something different was headed at them quickly. They were not headed for the drop zone they had anticipated but a different one on the opposite side of sprawling Ft. Campbell.

Unaware of the change in destination, they were soon following the instructions of the jumpmaster. They made a tight stick as they flew from the plane only to be snatched back toward it as the chutes were yanked open by the static line connected to the plane. Soon they were enjoying the view of central Kentucky and Tennessee from a perspective that everyone should appreciate once in their life.

As they hit the ground, the routine of recovering their chutes was now entering their muscle memory, and they hardly thought about their chores, so routine was the action. Ash was the first to comment, "Boy, I was getting nervous about that tree line." He nodded toward a bramble thicket barely a football field's length from them. "It seems every day we get dumped into a tighter DZ. I guess this is to develop our self-confidence in getting these things to put us down where we want to be."

As they approached the tree line, once again, they found the staff sergeant they had come to know as "the Watcher" alighting from his quarter-ton chariot. As usual, he was armed with the obligatory packet and the noon meal consisting of C rations. This was exactly as the previous day. Handing the packet to Ash, he started back to the jeep.

Ash surprised him, though, when he said, "Staff Sergeant, is there anything about this area that you can tell us that might make our task a little easier?"

He looked at them like a mule eating briars and said, "Remember, not everything is as it seems." With that, he was off and away from them. They would see no more of him from that point on. The previous day's escapade had cost him dearly in personal collateral with his boss, the NCOIC who was still stinging over the arrival of his students at an empty pack shed. The Watcher would be paying them very close attention today but from unobtrusive environs. He was pretty certain that he would not lose them again today nor jump to conclusions about their course of actions, which might lead to inaccurate reports being filed back at HQs. He wanted to become a first-class sergeant someday, and he knew the quickest way to ensure that he would not make it was to allow his boss to be embarrassed again.

Ash pointed to Wiznewski. "Get up on that hill and see which way he goes if you can." His instructions were barely out of his mouth when Wiz took off up the hill. In a few moments, he was back.

"The trail empties out on a road about fifty yards down the trail. He pulled across the road and is sitting down there waiting for us, I guess." Wiz was slightly winded from the rush up and down the hill.

Ash was sizing up the situation. The jump had left them in a much smaller LZ than the ones they had landed in on their previous jumps. But something didn't seem right about where they were located. The area was devoid of natural or man-made landmarks from which to get an orientation. Finally, he shot a back azimuth to the orientation of the LZ and set his bearing to bring them toward the pack shed. As they hustled down the trail, he was still uneasy about their course. After about fifteen minutes, he called a halt and immediately pulled out the map. Calling the group together, he proclaimed, "I think that we are going the wrong way. Look at this." He pointed to a symbol on the map. "You should see a fence running about 1,500 yards from the DZ we were supposed to land in. We haven't seen any fence running anywhere like that. Nuckles, I keep thinking about you saying they would drop us in the wrong place. I think that is just what they did." He looked at the map again. "I haven't been able to figure out where we actually are." He added this as he looked around the circle of faces.

Nuckles took the map and, turning it ninety degrees, pointed to a DZ on the opposite side of post. "Last night, when we were going over the route, I kind of did a rough map recon of the area. This DZ over here resembles the one we were told we would hit the closest of any I could spot. If you look, I believe we are about here, we just came around that curve back there in the trail," he said as he pointed to features on the map sheet. "Also, we are two isoclines above the drop zone here, and we have risen constantly since we left the DZ."

Ash looked around again. "Anyone else got a theory?" He was working hard to include everyone in the decision-making process. There was no reply from anyone.

Finally, Ash said, "Well, after yesterday, we will follow Nuckles's hunch at least until we see something that says we were wrong."

As they sat there at the rest halt, Ash worked out the route they would need to take to get back into the pack shed area the quickest they could. When they started off, they were going perpendicular to their march route previously used. They had to take some detours to avoid impact areas of some of the rifle ranges in the area, but they made good time and were standing outside the pack shed at 1600.

Today there were cadre members there to let them into the facility. They made quick work of repacking their chutes according to standards and were soon sitting in the conference room ready for the following day's briefing. The NCOIC opened the session by reviewing the day's activities. One of the first questions was, "How long did it take to figure out you had been dropped in the wrong place?"

Ash spoke up quickly, "Nuckles told me this morning you would do that to us. From the moment your staff sergeant left us, I was feeling like something was wrong. I looked for the fence that we should have come to about 500 yards from the DZ. When we didn't hit it after about 1,500 yards, I knew we were off target. That's when we figured out we were on the other side of BFE, and Nuckles helped me lay out our course. Of course, as you know, we had to avoid the impact areas of the ranges out there."

The NCOIC nodded. "We wanted you to know that the air force usually gets you close to where you need to be, but not always. Then we wanted to see your reaction. You all got attaboys for that one. That was about as quick as I have ever seen anyone figure out that problem. Good work."

"Now for tomorrow, expect to hit the DZ bright and early in the morning. You will need to be here no later than 0600. We have an early riser special for you tomorrow. He laid out the area for them, and after a few questions, they were ready for the jaunt back to their barracks.

They were ready to huddle up and break down the mission. After about ten minutes, they realized that either there wasn't enough information, or they were being given a really simple problem for their assignment. Either way, they all headed for the showers.

The next day, arising at 0500, they were standing in the chow line 0530. Each man grabbed a sausage biscuit and a carton of milk, and they were on their way. They were at the pack shed by 0545 and ready for the activities of their fourth jump. As they secured the equipment prepared by them the previous day, there was a tension in the air as they considered the simplicity of the mission they had been given.

As the C-141 left the runway, the four men comprising the first stick of jumpers were seated in the side, facing seats nearest the rear ramp of the cargo plane. As the light came on, they rose, hooked into the static line rail, and shuffled to the back of the plane. As the jumpmaster made the requisite contact with the parts of their equipment, they each pushed the thoughts of the mission to the back of their minds. As they approached the jump point, Ash realized that he could not get out of the plane today. Grabbing Wiznewski by the pack on his back, he whispered, "I can't go today. My nerves won't take it."

Wiznewski nodded and held his hand. As they approached the open ramp, Wiznewski suddenly had Ash's arm locked in his tightly grasping fist. As Wiznewski stepped off the ramp, Ash had no choice. He was coming out the back of the plane with Wiznewski. Once they were airborne, Wiznewski relaxed his grip on Ash's arm and let the momentum of the fall separate them. By the time the static line popped the chute out of its container, there was sufficient space between them for both chutes to deploy fully. Soon they were descending peacefully toward the ground. Ash was extremely pale. As he touched the ground, he deposited what was left of the breakfast he had put away that morning on the DZ's landing area. As they looked around, they noticed that, once again, the size of the DZ had grown smaller, but this did not bother them as they were becoming increasingly confident in their ability to get the chute to deliver them to the appointed destination. They simply had yet to encounter the vagaries of the weather.

As they began to secure their gear, Ash walked over to Wiznewski. "Why did you pull me out of the plane?" He demanded in an agitated voice. The others sensed danger in the voice, and the banter of the post-jump excitement was suddenly wiped away.

Wiznewski spread his hands out, palms up. "I was under the impression that we made a pact about a week back that if we could, we would have no cold feet in this outfit." Wiznewski answered shortly and turned to walk away. Now it was Ash's turn to grab his arm. In doing so, he spun the larger Wiznewski into him. The two leaned into each other for a few seconds and, Foster and Nuckles headed for the confrontation.

"Where do you think you're going?" Ash threw at them over his shoulder, never taking his eyes off Wiznewski. "This is between us. Let it be so."

Foster broke in before Ash could go any further, "This is not between the two of you. If you have forgotten, we have the Watcher over behind that tree line. Furthermore, we are under your command right now, Mr. Platoon Guide. You better get it through your head that we are trying to help you through a rough spot. If you don't, count on explaining to the major what the hell is bothering you."

While Foster was making this statement, Nuckles was maneuvering between the two men. He was now in position to keep them apart if they really didn't want to escalate the situation. Fortunately, the reign of common sense seemed to return.

Ash looked sheepishly at Wiznewski. "I know you saved my chance to get through this. Thanks for your help." He grabbed the other man's hand, they shook, and soon they were headed to the tree line with all equipment secure and accounted for. As they double-timed across the DZ, they all wandered what had happened? They didn't know that something of this nature seemed to occur in almost every iteration of jump school. It seemed strange to them because this was their first moment of conflict.

Upon reaching the tree line, they were greeted by a real surprise. The Watcher was not waiting for them by himself today. There parked next to his sedan was a cattle car. After a short review on the spot of the jump, they were loaded into the cattle car and driven in style back to the jump school's packing shed. Upon their arrival, they fell into the routine of preparing the equipment for tomorrow's jump. After finishing with this, they wordlessly moved into the conference room for the after-action review and the brief for the next jump.

The brief was short and to the point. Their final jump would include the cadre of the ranger school; all thirty-two men would jump together. This would be the first time they had jumped as a unit. Stidham had wanted to do this and had made special arrangements for the men to jump together. As the students came from the conference room, they saw the balance of the team busily packing chutes. They would have plenty of company tomorrow.

That evening in the barracks, they finally had some alone time to discuss the confrontation from earlier in the day. It was remarkable that not one person had brought up what had happened during any of their time with cadre from both the schools throughout the day. They simply wanted it to stay on the team at this point. From comments that had been made, it was obvious that both Stidham and the jump school NCOIC had strong suspicions about what had happened; but up until now, neither had been able to confirm those suspicions.

Ash broke the silence. Looking at Wiznewski, he commented, "I think I owe you a huge thank you, and I really am sorry for what happened on the ground."

Wiz looked at him and then said, "No apology needed, but it is accepted. Can I ask you one thing?"

Ash nodded and Wiz continued, "Were you really considering giving up on the mission? Or for that matter, giving up on us?"

Ash grinned. "I hadn't thought about it like that at all. So many things were building inside my head. I felt like I had to get away from it. I didn't want to quit, but I wasn't ready to jump. At least I didn't think I was. I know that had I not jumped today, I probably would have lost my spot on the team. Right now that's the only thing in the world that I feel like I belong to."

Foster interjected, "Have you had bad news from home?"

Ash grunted, "No, there isn't anyone back there to hear from. I know that all of us come from backgrounds that we are unlikely to have a cheering section greet us at the airport when we go home, if we go home, but it really got to me today. You guys have straightened me out. Thanks again for your help."

The tension had eased from the room during the conversation. They each reflected on how close they had come to losing a team member that day. Each man dealt with it in his own way. But none failed to reach a conclusion about that day's training.

The next day, they were up at 0500, doing their PT and taking care of the personal stuff that soldiers do every day. By 0630, they were entering the pack shed where they were greeted by the balance of the ranger school cadre. Securing their individual equipment, they were soon on their way to the green ramp. On this day, they had no wait for their C-141 was pulling to the gate area even as they arrived.

"That's service with a smile," Ash observed as he set the jump order for their jump. He was somewhat startled when Stidham came over and asked him, "Could you let Top go first today? Then I will follow you, if that is okay with you, I mean."

Ash was taken aback. Here was a field grade officer who could have easily ordered him to do what he wanted, being really considerate and recognizing his position in the school team; but most importantly, he was doing all this without emitting any air of condescension at all. Ash quickly nodded his approval. He didn't try to answer verbally. He wasn't sure that he could have gotten any words out at that point.

They clambered into the cargo area of the transport and found their seats. Shortly, they were under way. It seemed only seconds until the Christmas light at the exits were lit, signifying time to get ready, and each man began to worry about his own contribution to this endeavor.

Soon, the jumpmaster was patting down First Sergeant VunCanon, and he was out the rear ramp, followed closely by Nuckles, Wiznewski, Foster, and Ash. For this jump, the team had organized into three sticks, the first ten in number 1, and then eleven in each of 2 and 3. As the men floated toward the ground, they had a few moments to consider the shape of the world they were coming back into, and then they were on the ground, and the securing of the gear became the all-important preoccupation of each man.

When all was secure, they formed up as a unit, with the four students in the front. The NCOIC of the jump School came out of the tree line where he had been waiting. Called forward by Stidham, he then called the four newest paratroopers in the army forward. He said a few words about their accomplishments and then, with Stidham's assistance, presented jump wings to each man and impressed them on their chest. This time, honored tradition of the army airborne drew a few drops of blood; but what the heck, they had probably bled more when they were eight years old and became blood brothers with a dear friend with whom they no longer had any contact. They were also presented with their first beret, a lovely maroon one.

Stidham groaned when he saw the berets. He knew they were entitled to them and had earned the right to wear them. But he had never considered that these men would wear any beret except the black ranger emblem. He was a little disappointed but was too professional to ever let it show.

Calling for VunCanon to come forward, he instructed the first sergeant to move the men over to the tree line where the ubiquitous cattle car awaited. With congratulations ringing in the air, the men jovially mounted the truck and prepared to return to the school. It was not long before the more astute geographers among them knew they were not headed for the school.

It was only about fifteen minutes before they were sitting on the rifle range that Stidham had shown to Bringle on that day several weeks prior. Stidham had arranged for Cansler to meet them at the range with a truck laden with four rifle racks, thirty-two M16 A1s securely locked into them, and with sufficient ammunition to start a major regional conflict.

The team was quickly broken in two firing orders. There were sixteen firing points on the firing line. The personnel who conducted firing exercises for the CBT school were present, and they were soon launching bullets down range. As the first firing order came off the line, Nuckles was muttering to no one in particular. When Captain Mizell noticed him, he walked over and asked, "PV2 Nuckles, is there something wrong?"

Nuckles ruefully considered before answering, "Sir, we haven't been issued weapons yet, and we certainly haven't had the opportunity to zero these. Well, you see, sir, I actually missed two three-hundred-yard targets today. My daddy would tan my hide for wasting so much lead."

Mizell could not help but smile. "While I know we are getting printouts from today, this range is essentially an experimental range. They are still working on the sensors for the scoring points. They have not validated it for record fire at this time. You may not have missed those two shots. We will be getting you the opportunity to zero that weapon, but I would say firing expert with a weapon that hasn't been zeroed is quite an accomplishment."

Nuckles seemed visibly relieved but left with the observation, "I hope we get that zero before next Friday."

Mizell knew that he would have one of the trainees on his team when they went to the practical field problem. He knew at that moment which one was going to be his. This young man had found a home.

By 1400, everyone had fired, and the scores had been pondered, argued, and discarded as the case may be. The team assumed they would be moving back to the cantonment area when they were loaded up on the cattle car. When they simply moved across the range road to another area, there were knowing looks passed among the more veteran team members. When they were assembled, Stidham stood before them. "Some of you have had the opportunity to view up close the work of Sergeant First Class DeWitt and his fellow conspirators. Some have not had this opportunity. Now you have."

Calling DeWitt forward, Stidham related how the first-class sergeant had taken the photos of DUC Lo and translated them into the structures before them. For the team members who had actually seen the photos of the Vietnamese compound, the similarity was amazing. For those who had not been privy to the photos, a whole new world was about to be revealed. As they walked around the compound, DeWitt explained the interconnectedness of the structures and, to the best of his knowledge, the uses for which they were built. Occasionally, as questions were brought to him, he would turn to Stidham or Abramson and ask them to answer the why questions.

Before long, they had exhausted their first round of curiosity. The men began to fall silent. Finally, Sergeant Gibson, who had been having the time of his life submitting requisitions for supplies that were never denied, looked over at Major Stidham and asked, "Sir, are we to the point where we can begin to find out why we were brought here?"

Stidham considered for a moment and then said, "Men, we cannot conduct a briefing on this subject out here on range road. Let's reconvene back in the common area when we get back there. First Lieutenant Abramson, would you make the area ready for such a briefing?"

"Yes, sir," replied the young lieutenant who had been so instrumental in getting these men on board for this operation. He immediately started mentally through his checklist for preparation of a secure briefing area. He was pretty certain that this would be the first use of the security clearances these men had brought with them to the school.

Upon arrival back at the schoolhouse, the transformation of the common area into a briefing room had taken about ten minutes. Setting up butcher block chart paper, photo display racks and blacking out the windows were quickly accomplished. Then First Sergeant VunCanon wheeled into the room from a little-used storage closet, a surprise even to Stidham. There was an incredibly detailed sand table depicting the area they had come to know as Duc Lo, even down to piano wires running across to make the map grids.

"Courtesy of Captain Jamison and his men." The first sergeant was quick to give credit to the team that had taken such care in building this immaculate training device. The mood in the room was intense as the entire team for the first time prepared to hear the details of the mission they would soon engage upon.

"Let me tell you what I know about the mission so far," Stidham began his talk as if he were at a Sunday school meeting, not a top-secret national defense briefing. "This facility"—and he indicated the first of the Duc Lo photos—"has been active for some time as a way station for American POWs being transported to the Hanoi Hilton. There have been at least three iterations of prisoners through here in the past ten weeks. We have been monitoring the site by use of U-2 technology. We have accepted the challenge of relieving the next group of prisoners to come through here. Normally, they seem to hold the prisoners here for about four to six days before moving them into Hanoi. There are usually four to eight men held here at a time. This facility is only about nineteen miles from Hanoi. If we can pull this off, think of the suffering we can save those men who won't get to enjoy the amenities of the Hilton. Captain Jamison, I am sure that you can give us an up-to-date estimate of the local terrain."

Captain Jamison was on his feet and, just as Stidham had expected, was quickly filling in the terrain features, the meteorological data, and the connecting transport routes into and out of the area. It was obvious that his team had been doing some intense research both in the library and from their knowledge of the Southeast Asia region. The matter-of-fact presentation soon had the four newest Airborne Paratroopers feeling like this must be commonplace for these men they were about to attempt to join.

"As you can imagine," Stidham began, "we will develop a plan for a multiprong advance on the facility and attempt to take it over with a minimum of violence. We obviously want to keep the bullets to an absolute minimum. We don't want to make it worse for the guests being housed here."

At this point, he turned to the new men in the group, "You may or may not know this, but every man on this team except for you four has completed at least one year in country (spent a year in Vietnam). They have served in the rangers or the predecessors of the rangers, and they have served with me for at least one tour. I can vouch for them. They are the best men I have ever served with in my eighteen years in the military. Listen to them, and your odds of making it through this mission increase dramatically. And by the way, it is now too late to back out of this training. Welcome aboard."

This brief overview of what was to come overshadowed any plans for a major celebration of the group's completion of airborne school. They did decide to go to the EM club on post for the evening mill. They had all returned to the barracks by 2200. A dose of reality goes a long way toward curing the urge to celebrate when one has reached an intermediate goal. Ten weeks before, they would have been overjoyed at what they had accomplished in such a short period. Now it was just a mile marker on the way to their ultimate goal—being a part of the release of a group of American POWs. They were stoked to be part of this grand mission.

On Saturday, by 0630, they were up and investigating the posted training schedule for the next week. They were in for a busy week. There was an intense hand-to hand combat session on Monday, a land navigation and orienteering session on Tuesday, Wednesday showed an introduction into Chinese conversational speech, and on Thursday there would be an introduction into nonlethal weaponry and its usage. Of course, Friday held the weekly firing session and operational training at the mock-up village they now knew as Duc Lo.

After perusing this, Ash looked over at Wiznewski, grinned, and ripped the scabbard off his shoulder denoting the platoon guide for the week. "What a pleasure to get to present this to you, in an unofficial way, of course. For a while, I didn't think I would last out the week. Thanks for your help, and good luck during your turn at this." With that, he handed over the symbol of leadership that each would bear on a rotating basis during the course of the training.

Week 3

Dallas 7–St. Louis Cardinals 20
Baltimore 14–Boston Patriots 6

On Monday, the men began with their obligatory PT session. With Wiznewski sliding into the PG slot, there was hardly any notice of the change. Things were going smoothly. They moved into the prescribed area for the hand-to-hand combat training. It would be safe to say that they were all shocked by the intensity of the first hour of training. While not antagonistic toward any one of the group, when they were turned over to Staff Sergeant Evans and his assistant Sergeant Galbreath, they were soon wondering if they would survive the instruction. To say the instruction was hands-on would be like saying the Pope has strong religious beliefs. These men had been in the far-out reaches of Vietnam, on some days probably not in the actual country, and had often relied on their skills with the body to get them out of tight spots in which they seemed to find themselves. The basic tenets of hand-to-hand they had been exposed to in CBT were exhausted in the first ten minutes. Then they moved on to highly efficient techniques for getting the opponent neutralized. They spent the balance of the first hour on these skills.

After a quick ten-minute break, the subject matter experts (SME), as they came to be known, brought them back into the circular area and began a session on how to eliminate the opposition if the situation demanded it. Their primary consideration was the level of force necessary to bring about effective results. During the third hour, they moved on to selection of targets for maximum effects. They might know if a particular opponent possessed information they needed to continue their mission. These techniques were designed to select the appropriate member of the opposition to give that particular target a view of what could happen to him if they so desired. They were considerably relieved to find out that the decision of who fell into this target designation would almost always be the discretion of the team's senior leaders.

After a break for chow, they moved on to practice against the dummies that the supervisory team had arranged to use and deploy at them as they moved through the area. Without realizing it, they had begun to conduct multifunctional training with emphasis placed on a particular area, but they were sharpening other survival skills concurrently. This aspect of their training would be emphasized in coming days in an even-more-demanding manner.

By the end of the day, they were approaching exhaustion. As they double-timed back to their barracks, there was no thought of anything except to get some rest. They had embarked upon the most physically demanding aspect of the training, which would sustain them through the arduous tasks they would be assigned to perform in future missions.

On Tuesday morning, they were moving at considerably less-than-top speed during their morning PT. As they approached the halfway mark of their two-mile run, they were surprised to see Stidham and VunCanon waiting for them as they came around a bend in the trail Wiznewski had laid out for them the night before. How the senior leaders knew they would be coming around that particular bend did not occur to them at the time. It was a real morale boost for them that they had shown up at that moment. The pace quickened, and the level of enthusiasm being exhibited took a definite positive turn. Stidham and VunCanon exchanged knowing glances, realizing that they had earned their keep for that day by simply being out on the trail.

As they finished breakfast and secured their barracks for the day, they had reached the peak of their enthusiasm and eagerness to undertake the day's activities. The land navigation and orienteering course was laid out and waiting for them. Nuckles had thought he would be well ahead of the curve on this set of tasks. He was certainly surprised when Abramson and DeWitt began to talk about ranger beads. DeWitt, in his spare time, had made each of the newly awarded trainees a set of the ranger beads. Consisting of braided parachute cords and ten large black beads, the innocuous-looking beads were vital to every ranger's kit. Normally they were worn on the uniform blouse.

As he handed each of them their set of beads, DeWitt began to explain their function. They were vital to pace counting and served as a kind of abacus for keeping up with the number of paces moved. He then explained that with a measured stride, the effective ranger could cross a standard grid square in one thousand paces. Every one hundred paces called for one bead to be advanced to the other end of the braided cord. In this way, there was a check and balance when they had reached one thousand paces. They could check the map for nearby terrain or man-made features to ensure that their directional progress was on target.

DeWitt moved on to obstacle avoidance by counting paces around the obstacle, shooting a back azimuth before going around the object and then reestablishing the direction on the other side. He went into the intricacies of terrain and man-made features and the use of the compass and stars to move, especially at night. Then he moved on to establishing eight-digit grid coordinates for points on the map. Then he went into how these could be used for calls for fire support.

As the men heard the lessons being taught, it began to dawn on them that this day would not be ending at 1700 or at any time soon after that. They intuitively knew they would be applying these tasks during an evening exercise. They were not disappointed. When they saw Gibson heading their way with C rations for their evening meal, their suspicions were confirmed. They were released from the class at about 1400, with instructions to report back at 1800. They were given twelve sets of grid coordinates, a map, and a compass to conduct their exercise.

For the purposes of the exercise, they were broken into two-man teams. Nuckles and Foster comprised the first team, and Ash and Wiznewski made up the second team. To ensure that they operated independently of each other, the points had been interspersed between the teams in the order that they were to be found. The team 3 cadre members were placed at strategic points throughout the exercise area to further ensure that the teams were in fact operating independently. An individual item had been placed at each point, which was to be brought back by each team to assure that they had in fact found the points that were described. To increase the competitive edge, each team had put up $5 that they would be back first. The teams were allotted four hours to complete the course. Unknown to them, much larger sums were being laid out by the senior instructors who had pegged Wiznewski and Ash as the early favorites. They had based their odds on the fact that Foster had asked a number of questions over again even after receiving the instructions. Nuckles had not shown any great interest in the topic, which, they had assumed, meant that he would not be effective at performing them. Apparently, they had not heard of his prowess in this area, or perhaps they were assuming that the level of expertise called for here would exceed his ability.

Nuckles and Foster completed the cross-country course at 2215. Wiznewski and Ash came in about five minutes behind them. There was some good-natured banter between the two teams. As they were released for the evening, they headed for the barracks. As the team of trainees walked away, a goodly amount of money was changing hands. Also changing was the perception of some of these veteran soldiers of the capabilities of these young troops. For the first orienteer exercise, they had done better than the average normally experienced by young soldiers.

They slept in the next day, rising at 0630. They were assembled in the classroom by 0800. They were wondering who the SME would be as they moved into the classroom. They were really surprised when it turned out to be Sergeant Williams, the junior member of the veteran component of the team. He explained that there were a number of variations of the Chinese language and that he was fluent to a certain level in the Mandarin dialect. This was the most common strain of Chinese spoken in the South Vietnamese region. He wasn't sure if that held true for the North, but they had to assume that it was true. Really all they had to do was learn enough to listen to overheard conversations. By the end of the day, they had learned fifteen common sentences that they hoped they would never get the opportunity to use.

On Thursday, they were back in the saddle for Sergeant First Class DeWitt and his nonlethal weapons class. It was amazing the number of common objects that could be used to subdue an opponent. The first-class sergeant went into how, in many situations, they would need to bring an opponent into submission while being able to question him or his cohorts. The techniques that could be used for these purposes were thoroughly explained and explored.

Any tendency they might have exhibited to nonchalant this portion of the training was quickly negated when they were placed in the hands-on positions of applying the techniques to one another. There were also dummy practices for a number of the techniques, which, if correctly applied, could result in personal injury. Almost all of them, if applied incorrectly, could have had that same type of result. Even with the protective personal gear that was supplied, they still quickly learned a healthy respect for the seriousness of the subject matter. They were a rapt group for the good sergeant's presentation but even more so for the portion of the class when they demonstrated their mastery of the topics involved.

By the time they broke up for the evening, they were tired and excited about the level of training they had received not only for that day but also through this portion of the first week. They were really getting to be gung ho as the saying went. Next they would be calling one another lifers. This was one of the things that separated the young soldiers from the veterans. The older men had committed to the military as a way of life. The young men considered it the least likely outcome they could imagine for their lives. They had no way of knowing how closely they were walking the line of becoming committed the same as their proctors.

By Friday, they were primed to participate in the weekly firing exercise. This week, they were taken to the zero range, where they had the opportunity to hone in their M16A1 rifles. The rifles were soon zeroed and ready for the record range. Stidham had chuckled again at the thought of the young Nuckles so upset over missing two targets the week before.

As the first firing order came off the line, he saw why the long face the week prior. The four young team members had recorded three perfect scores and one thirty-nine of forty. Still, Stidham mused how many men had he seen that could hit any target presented but wilted when faced with a living breathing opponent on the battleground. He was not above using their performance to motivate the more experienced members of his team, but there were precious few misses being recorded there either.

After everyone on the team completed the firing range, the entire team moved to the mock-up of the Duc Lo compound. The four young members had not yet been integrated into their portion of the exercise. The arrival of the four quarter-ton vehicles into the area signaled that this was about to be rectified. First Sergeant VunCanon had assumed responsibility for bringing them up to speed on their responsibility.

One of the first topics brought up was the possibility of mounting Ma Deuces (M2, fifty-caliber machine guns) on the vehicles. Stidham had already arrived at the conclusion that this would not be necessary and might take up valuable space needed to evacuate any disabled POWs that they might get out. He did however, allow the members of the team to discuss the possibility of mounting this weaponry on the vehicles. After about thirty minutes of give-and-take among the senior members of the team, they had independently come to the same conclusion. Because of the topography of the area, there would be limited utility to the addition of the weapon systems, and the loss of utility for transporting released POWs would not justify this small advantage. Stidham smiled as he realized that he had not had to spend any of his command credits to get his point across. As VunCanon gazed over at Stidham, the team leader spoke. "Is there something on your mind, Top?"

"Well, sir, I was thinking that rather than attaching these men one to each team, it might be worth considering leaving them unattached." The first sergeant was still putting his final thoughts to this line of reasoning. He was not committed to this as a final say-so but was seeking to justify the idea he had developed. "You see, sir, there are not good access routes from all directions into the compound. If we only bring the vehicles from one direction we have only one route to secure, the drivers can still be responsible for a particular team's release point. We may have missed this if we hadn't had the sand table that the guys built. Looking at that thing made me realize that what we have been developing out here may not be as realistic as we thought." The first sergeant paused, thinking ahead to any objections he might have to overcome.

"Top, I think you may have hit on something there." Stidham was supportive of the thought process the older man had embarked upon and was trying to provide as much push as possible. "They would be more central to the entire operation and could be reactive to the flow of developing situations from that vantage point." As VunCanon finished his thought, it came to Stidham that he had seen an alignment taking shape between individuals and certain team leaders. These would have to be overcome for the good of the team if they adopted VunCanon's strategy. Still, he was leaning to this new employment technique as he thought about the possible ramifications for their mission.

That evening, after training was complete at the mock-up site, the team held their usual debriefing session. Gathered around the sand table, they watched as the junior team members recounted the actions of their sections. Then the leaders responded to the suggestions that the lower-ranking men had laid out. This bottom-up review provided several points that had to be cleared up. Some demonstrated the failure of communications to be clearly passed through the chain of command, some were the result of the guy on the ground seeing what needed to be done more clearly than the guy who made the plan, and some were simply the result of men not understanding what the interactions of efforts were designed to produce. All were addressed, and those that could be solved were handled. None were referred to a committee.

The junior members of the team were dismissed to return to their quarters, while the leadership met for a discussion of the coming week's agenda. They were all impressed by the progress that the new trainees had exhibited through this point, but they realized that these men were a long way from ready for the rigors of what was to come. The training plan was amped up to reflect their determination to accomplish what must be done.

Week 4

Dallas 13–Atlanta 0
Baltimore 23–Houston Oilers 10

The following week began with the roll out for PT. Nuckles was in the position of platoon guide for the week. He soon realized that he had been chosen for the most challenging physical week of the training to date. After their workout, they fell out with full ALCE (army load carrying equipment) known as Alice packs and full-battle rattle. They were going cross-country.

When First Lieutenant Scandretti handed him the frag order for the mission, he knew he faced a severe leadership challenge. His mission was to move from point to point, observe activities at each point, leave an observer at that point, move to the next point, observe, etc. Each point was located about three to four miles between points. There were four points, so following the progression, he would be the only soldier moving to the last point. There was no way to bypass points to acquire all points simultaneously.

He sat the men down and went over the mission. They were expected to cross the SP (start point) in one hour. He had some time to get everyone's thoughts. Scanning the map, they noticed that the first point was a ranger station out on range road. The second point was in the middle of nowhere, with no prominent manmade objects reflected on the map. The third point was an ammunition storage facility. The fourth point was the post marshaling yard for staging equipment about to be deployed.

Talking quietly, they came up with a simple plan. They would all move to point 1 and observe for fifteen minutes. Wiznewski would remain at this point and continue the observation. The remainder of the team would move to point 2, observe for a like time, and try to figure out what they were to observe and then leave Foster at this point. Ash and Nuckles would then move to point 3, observe, and Ash would remain, while Nuckles moved on to point 4. They had each been issued a C ration for the noon meal. Nuckles instructed them to eat at their own volition and in tune with whatever activity was being observed.

By the time they had fleshed out the plan, it was approaching time to hit the SP. They actually crossed the SP about a minute and a half early. They were about forty-five minutes in reaching the ranger station. As they were acquiring a vantage point that provided cover but unimpeded access, they saw a TMP (transportation motor pool) sedan pull to the front of the station. The three occupants of the sedan went inside. As they reached the front door, they were met by an inhabitant of the building they had not been aware was on the inside. For the next ten minutes, there was no further activity at the site. Leaving Wiznewski at the site, the other three team members moved out to the second point.

Again, they were on the move for about forty-five minutes. Calling a halt, Nuckles told them, "I'm not certain, but as close as I can tell there is a firebreak that intersects this tank trail at these coordinates. I believe right over this hill will put us in close proximity to that point. We don't want to cross the hill but keep our profiles behind the horizon and get where we can see the point." Nodding, the other two swung their gear back up on their shoulders and eased up the hill. Arriving a little short of the crest, they peered over the crown of the ridge; and sure enough, there was the junction of the firebreak and tank trail that Nuckles had described. For several minutes, nothing moved in either direction. Nuckles was beginning to doubt his selection of the point. Suddenly, they noticed a group of soldiers moving down the firebreak recklessly but quickly. Shortly, they came to a halt, put out guards, and then began to eat their C rations. Foster looked at Nuckles and grinned. "I guess I get to watch the feast of the Passover."

Nuckles chuckled back and said, "Just hope they pass over your position out here. Ash and I have to move on to our points now." With that, they slid down the backside of the ridge they had occupied and began their trek to the third point. Once again, it required forty-five minutes of hard marching to arrive near by the ASP (ammunition supply point). Pausing to get their bearings, Ash had a thought, "Did that frag order say what part of the ASP we were to watch?"

Nuckles looked at the paper he had been given. "No, it says watch the ammo point."

"Well, that ammo point is behind six feet of mesh wire topped by concertina, probably two or three strands," Ash surmised. "I think the best place to see the most is on this side." He indicated the area on the map they had made a part of their equipment. Nuckles saw why he picked that area. There was a good sight line from the heavily wooded area across the street that allowed a view of both the incoming traffic and the outgoing movement as well. "They didn't specify what we were looking for, so I think you're right."

Being right was a good thing; being on the opposite side of the facility was not. They had to spend an extra ten minutes working their way around the exterior of the perimeter to get into the selected position. Once there, they noticed that this was a heavily traveled route. "Make sure we don't miss anything here." Nuckles was talking to both himself and Ash as he settled into the viewing spot they had selected. Suddenly, they saw the TMP sedan they had observed at point 1 pull into the facility.

At first, there was no recognition; but when the occupants dismounted to move indoors, Ash grunted triumphantly, "That's the guys who were at the ranger station getting out of that sedan. The guy in the backseat, I know I recognize him."

"Good going, but don't go to sleep out here. There may be more action coming here." Nuckles was relieved that they would at least have something to report that seemed connected to the other points. "I have to get going if I'm to make it to my point on time." With that, he was off.

One advantage to his move was that he could move faster through the brush by himself than they had as a group. He actually arrived a little ahead of the time specified. He found a vantage point allowing him visual of the entire marshaling area, but especially the ingress and egress routes of the area. After several minutes, he noticed a two-and-a-half-ton truck moving into the area. There were only a handful of vehicles in the area, and from his work as an operator of military vehicles, he was glad they were not his responsibility to get on the road. They looked really sad. Then he noticed the truck discharging troops from the cargo compartment. They were familiar. He knew he had seen at least two of them at point 2, but were they all there, or was this some of the same? He knew he had failed this task.

His order told him to observe for thirty minutes and then begin to retrace his route to retrieve his team members. After watching for the prescribed interval, he hit the trail. Moving quickly, he soon arrived back at Ash's position. Questioning him, he felt his heart flutter. Ash had only generalizations to report. He knew that they would not get good marks at this point either.

They moved back the way they had come and soon were coming upon Foster. He had a report that a two-and-a-half-ton truck had come along and picked up the soldiers who had stopped for lunch at the junction he was watching. "How many soldiers were there?" Nuckles questioned.

Grinning like a Cheshire cat, Foster reached into his pocket and pulled out a sheet of paper he had torn from his always-present notepad. "I took the liberty while I was reclining here at the pass over to design a little form. It says there were twelve men in the detail we observed."

Nuckles looked at the form and realized he was on to something. "We need to incorporate this into any exercise like this. It's a really handy tool. We might want to enhance it a little." Without realizing it, he was making a prophet out of his football coach who had frequently told him and his team, "You are who you practice to be." He was becoming a clone of Stidham without even noticing the transformation.

They moved quickly back down the trail to Wiznewski, who reported that there must have been some kind of meetings going on in the ranger station because he had lost count of the comings and goings from there, but he did report that the three guys in the sedan who had triggered the day's activities had returned a short time ago, gone inside the station, and emerged a short time later. The inhabitant of the building was still there.

They moved back down the trail. As they moved along, Nuckles was contemplating the day's events. He was far from satisfied. He knew that he had made mistakes. He knew that the team had not achieved all they were expected to accomplish from this mission. He was actually looking forward to the period of debriefing.

As the team and the trainers gathered for the after-action briefing, Nuckles found Lieutenant Scandretti and, calling him to the side, asked, "Sir, may I have a minute with you?"

Scandretti looked at him and answered, "Certainly. What's on your mind?"

"Sir, I know we made mistakes today. I have some ideas about what we need to do to fix them. Would it be possible for me to get a chance at the fixing before the debriefing?"

Scandretti thought for a moment and then, shaking his head, said, "I appreciate that you want to fix the problems you see with what was done today. But we have a whole set of notes that we want to go over with you guys. I think it is entirely possible that some of the issues you were planning to fix are the same issues we will bring up, but I also think that we will bring up things that you may not have considered. I would ask you to listen to us before you start fixing problems that may be only half fixes for the issues that underlie the problems you see."

Nuckles was at first crestfallen to not be given an opportunity to fix what he felt he had messed up, but as he considered the officer's answer, the wisdom of this course of action dawned on him. He finally grinned and said, "I think I see what you're getting at. We just need one Mr. Fixit session for everything."

Scandretti nodded and went to the front of the room. The always-ready sand table stood waiting for its exercise. The lieutenant turned the session over to Sergeant First Class Taylor, who would conduct the debriefing. Turning to the team, he asked, "Why did you not request anything from us during the ramp-up period we provided you? We had glasses (binoculars), additional maps with overlays of possible enemy deployments. Radios were here that could have been utilized. You never raised the issue of how these objectives were interconnected, and there didn't seem to be an overall grasp of the mission as opposed to focusing on the individual pieces. Platoon Guide, could you respond to this?"

Nuckles looked over at Lieutenant Scandretti, nodded, and began, "Thank you, Sergeant First Class Taylor. I don't think we have had a previous mission where there were resources we needed that we had to request. Rather, they had always been given us. There was no mention in the frag order that the individual tasks might be interrelated. I did figure that out after we were out on the course when I saw the TMP vehicle show up at two points and when we recognized some of the soldiers from the point of the trail at the marshaling yard. Boy, those radios would have really come in handy then. The additional maps would also have been great so each soldier could have one at his point to make notations about the operation. Obviously, the glasses would have enabled us to get a lot more details about the points we were observing. I felt that we were able to see the points, but we didn't get enough details, such as the rank of the opposing force individuals, the makeup of the force at each point, and the bumper numbers of the vehicles or identifying characteristics of them. The overlays of the enemy activities would have been invaluable in assessing the overall mission. As a matter of information, if we had requested a full operational order, would we have received one?"

Taylor was caught off-guard by this question. His pawns had just become rooks in his game of chess, and they were showing signs of becoming even more powerful. "I will defer that question to the L-T." Thinking quickly, he nodded to Scandretti.

"As a matter of fact, there was a full OPLAN developed for this phase of the training. Whether we had it with us this morning is a different matter." Scandretti had answered the question without giving a direct response. Nuckles decided not to pursue this matter further; he had the balance of the week to endure with this team.

"As a matter of fact"—Nuckles was back on his feet and thinking ahead—"I had requested that we be given a period to review our actions before this meeting. I had several approaches in mind that now knowing that I wasn't restricted to what I had, we could have developed into a better plan. If we could have a second chance at this or a similar operation, I think we can improve significantly on our performance. Sir, is there a chance for a redo on this tomorrow?" With this, Nuckles sat down, waiting for a reply.

When the reply came, he was astonished. Scandretti looked over the team and said, "I don't know if the training schedule can be adjusted that much. We have several critical tasks coming up to train you guys on. Let me hear your discussion of changes you would make if we were going to allow you to retrain tomorrow."

Nuckles quickly assumed control of the discussion, "Well, sir, I think PV2 Wiznewski can do better at his observation tasks if I give him more detailed guidance of what we are looking for in his report. Since he was assigned to observe a fixed point, I should have made it a part of his responsibility to find out who the people were that came and went from the point, not simply that three parties comprised of twelve individuals came to the point during the time he was watching. Individual's ranks are key and, if possible, unit identifications would have been critical information to gather. If it was apparent that there was a rank structure, that would have been key information. Sir, at point 3, PV2 Ash developed a rough form that I would use at all points to record the information from each point. It may need some modification, but it is a good starting point for us to use." He indicated that Ash should share his form with the team. Foster and Wiznewski scanned the form and nodded, agreeing that this would have been an important tool they could have used. They quickly covered the adaptions they would make for their points to make the form user friendly for their tasks.

Moving on to Foster's coverage of the point where the two trails met, Nuckles stated, "I had no idea what we were looking for at this point. In retrospect, I know that it was important to know the amount of traffic and the direction that traffic was heading. Again, peripheral information on units and vehicles would have been key."

"Another thing," Foster was joining the conversation, "it would have been useful information to know that some of the traffic was uniting at that point. This seems to be a point where the enemy is consolidating their forces possibly."

Ash was ready to improve his performance. "I was at the ammo supply point. I counted vehicles and personnel going in, but there were times when I could plainly see what was being loaded into the various vehicles. I should have included this in my form. Sorry." He looked wistfully at Nuckles, who was taking a real beating in this debriefing.

Nuckles said, "At my point, I saw people coming and going around the vehicles in the marshaling yard. It never dawned on me to find out what activity related to those vehicles. Were they being prepared for shipping, were they preparing to move out tactically, or were they being sabotaged? I didn't find out any of these things. Any of which may have been crucial.

"As a leader, I should have found out the purpose for gathering the information so I could help each of my soldiers have a better idea of what was critical and how to perform the tasks they were assigned. Each of you would have benefitted from a better performance by me. Also, I now know not to be bashful about requesting resources. They might not be available, but if they are not asked for, the answer is automatically no. I should have known if we were gathering information for use on the spot or if that information would be transmitted up the chain through a SPOT Report. I think the intended user is a key element we have yet to consider. Also, how much time do we have, and how much can we safely use the radios to communicate between points?"

At this point, Scandretti interrupted the conversation. "You men just demonstrated what an after-action review is all about. Without thin skins or hurt feelings, you identified strengths and weaknesses in your operation and made suggestions for improving it on the next iteration.

Unnoticed until now, Stidham had slipped into the back of the room. He had sent VunCanon ahead of him to make sure that there was no calling of at ease if someone saw him enter. He wanted to observe both the trainers and the trainees. He was pleased by the thoroughness of the review but somewhat puzzled by sending these raw trainees out without a more detailed frag order. He was impressed with their growth into the roles they had played but concerned about the lack of competitive edge within the group. Rangers had always been type-A personalities, and he was afraid that this group might get swallowed up by this at some point. Still, it was impressive that he noticed some of the junior trainers looking surprised at some of the insights that the trainees were demonstrating. In his estimation, this was team building at its finest.

When the after-action review started to wind down, Nuckles looked up at Scandretti and said, "Well, sir, do we get another chance at this tomorrow?"

Scandretti smiled and shook his head. "Private Nuckles, I know you think you and your team can do better, and I appreciate that you grasp the gravity of doing things right. The bottom line is even though you see major areas you can improve upon, due to the time constraints we have and the level that you performed, we are giving you passing marks for these tasks. Furthermore, these tasks are building block tasks for areas to be trained further at a later date. We will continue with the published training schedule for tomorrow."

Nuckles, while disappointed to not get a second chance, knew that the team would improve its performance when those tasks were incorporated into the further exercises they would be engaging. He was unaccustomed to accepting less than perfection in his personal performance, and this stuck in his crawl a little bit.

As the trainees departed from the briefing area, Scandretti noticed Stidham motioning for him to come to his office. "Why would you give these guys this type of complex leadership issues to deal with when you know they have no background to build upon?" The major was not confrontational but inquisitive. He was sure that something had led to the thought process, and he sincerely wanted to understand the dynamics.

"Sir, I have had my eye on this young private since I got here. He has some of the best instincts for leading troops that I have ever seen. He is almost always one or more jumps ahead of the rest. I wanted to challenge him not to accept the routine of the tasks we gave him but to see the overall picture of the situation we were developing. Sir, he, along with his team, developed a great tool for documenting what they were observing while staying on task. That's innovative thinking at its finest. I think he performed terrifically. Sir, as long as we are talking, I would like to put in right now to have him assigned to my team, if that's how we are going to utilize these guys on our real-life mission."

Stidham relaxed at hearing the explanation of the training scenario. Now he had another area to concern him, but he was not ready to be painted into that corner yet. "I will keep your request in mind, but we are not anywhere near developing that thought process. Don't let me forget if we decide to employ them in that manner. And by the way, I like what you did to develop your leader. Always watch the leaders and learn from them, the good and the bad. Keep some, throw out some." With that, he rose and headed for the door. "Unless you have something else that won't keep overnight, I'm heading for my quarters."

Scandretti rose and went back to the common area where he sat and thought for a few minutes. Then he ambled over to the quarters area of the team. Spotting Nuckles and Foster on the front stoop of the building, he asked, "Not much going on this evening?"

"No, sir, just going over some of the events for tomorrow," Nuckles's reply came back. "I would sure not want to get caught unprepared for radio transmissions. Since we had a lesson today in how to better employ them, we will really see the need for them in our mission." Scandretti was searching for any hint of sarcasm in his voice or his body language. Seeing none, he surmised that he was getting honest feedback.

"Could I get a few moments with you to go over a few things?" He turned to Nuckles, indicating that he wanted to talk alone. Foster took the hint and, rising, moved into the barracks. "Let's walk this way." Scandretti indicated the direction he wished to go, but he smiled as he thought about the movie where the character had said something similar and the entire cast had mimicked his walk. Nuckles was not about to mimic the lieutenant.

"I wanted you to know that I was extremely impressed with your reactions out on the course today. As you saw things going downhill, you were proactive in coming up with ways to modify the situation. It was also impressive that you were not ready to let this event go with an 'Oh well, we'll do better next time.' I like the attitude and resourcefulness you have demonstrated. I want you to know that we kind of set you up for failure to see how you would handle it, not to make you look bad, but to let you know that life is not always coming up on a silver platter. I think you reacted superbly."

"Thank you, sir." Nuckles was considering his response. "Sir, I know that some of the men on your team would just as soon that we not be part of the mission. I understand that. But I want you to know that we didn't ask for this or seek it in any way. They came to us and asked us. We want to be good soldiers. We know this mission has to do with getting some POWs out of Vietnam. If we were there, we would want someone to come for us if they could. That's all we want to do, to get them out if we can. Could you please let your team know that? We want to help, not compete."

Scandretti looked at the young private who had simply, succinctly wrapped up the differences not only within the team but also within the society as a whole. Cooperation seemed to always lose out to competition at all levels. He had come out here to assure the younger man that he had done well during the day's training and come away with a deeper understanding of the society in which he lived.

He thought of mentioning his request to have Nuckles assigned to his team but decided not to mention it since it had not so far been approved. He knew that until it was officially noted that there could be other outcomes. He would leave it alone for now.

"Anyway, I wanted you to know that we are not down on you at all. We thought you were strong enough to face this type of situation without losing your confidence. Please show the entire team that we were right in our assessment of you and the team. You guys really have some terrific talents that we need to hone for the overall mission." Scandretti was earnest in his statement, and he knew that he needed to bring the young private off the fence post and into his camp. His actions would prove to do just that.

Speaking of time, he had to prepare to brief Barstow on his latest two trips. He was fast coming to the end of his burn. The pressure of the jet lag was really slowing him down. Pulling a legal pad from his briefcase, he began to list the important action items from both visits. He had placed a great heading at the top of the first page when he felt the stewardess awaken him to tell him to buckle up. They were beginning their descent into Dulles's traffic pattern. He had drifted off and slept throughout the entire flight. His trip through the baggage area and the retrieval of his car from long-term parking was uneventful as was his trip home.

The next morning, he was beginning to shake the cobwebs from his brain when he thought, *I never prepared my notes for Barstow.* Well, he had time when he arrived at Foggy Bottom for that. During his drive, he began to put together the elements of his report.

When he walked into the office reserved for him on the seventh floor, he was somewhat surprised at the note on the door. The ADO wanted to see him immediately. He was soon on the elevator going to the eleventh floor. He got off and went directly to Barstow's office, where he was waved in at once.

"Well, how did the meeting go in Paris?" Barstow was not inquiring about the agricultural involvement of the North Vietnamese but rather about the elements of the trip that had led him to initially send Bringle over there. He had not foreseen the possibility of involvement at the depth it had apparently sunk. He was quite honestly tempted to pull the plug but dad-blamed if he could see walking away from the chance to get a group of POWs out of there. The only thing better would be if he could get them out of the Hanoi Hilton. He didn't think that was likely, so he decided to play the hand he had been dealt.

Bringle quickly brought him up to date on the status of Dinh's providing the routing information for any payments to a Swiss bank account, the fact that no money had changed hands, and the request for more schedule information. Bringle went on to tell his boss of his recommendation that one more iteration of exchanges of prisoners go through Duc Lo before the rescue team be sent in.

With that out of the way, he switched gears to Stidham and his project. He filled in the gaps that were apparent from his knowledge of how the mission was taking place. He covered the planning of operations and hit on the preciseness of the preparations for the execution of the plan, the commander's concept of the operation, and the need that he foresaw of an extensive travel agenda for the team. As he saw it, there would be a requirement for several takeoffs aboard air force transports but few if any landings. He believed the flight crews would be free to return to their home base before they had completed any flight.

Barstow had begun to think that Stidham was probably the man for this task. He was overcoming every obstacle that was encumbering his team and, amazingly enough, not getting his feathers ruffled by Bringle, which Barstow realized was no small feat in and of itself. He knew from experience in his own bureaucratic world that oftentimes those attempting to help are the biggest hindrances. His esteem for Stidham was steadily growing. While he had never doubted the intentions of Bringle, he had often found his capabilities to be exceeded by the task he was asked to execute. He had to watch this operation closely. He couldn't let it blow up on this team or, for that matter, on the prisoners who might be affected by any misstep in this mission.

Bringle settled into a routine. Daily he was checking the flyover pictures first thing each morning, he was monitoring reports from Stidham, and he was maintaining his contacts at the Department of Agriculture while he waited for the next round of bilateral talks to be scheduled. He suspected that he would not have long to wait. He felt the crescendo of excitement building as more and more parts of the plan he had put into motion were made into reality.

Peter Carter came to his office on one morning during this time. He handed Brindle a file folder that had been logged into the NSA system back in May. Bringle was soon looking at a picture of an open area that seemed vaguely familiar, but he couldn't place where he had seen this area or the context in which he knew of it. Carter expectantly bided his time. Finally, Bringle looked over the folder at the analyst and said, "I'm drawing a blank here. Help me out."

Carter produced a second folder whose heading identified it as having been created in early July. Opening the folder, Bringle noted the now familiar compound they had come to refer to as Duc Lo. It slowly began to dawn on Bringle what the other folder had been. We were watching some nearby activity when we happened to pick up these coordinates. Six weeks later, when we went to shoot the same area, our pilot lost his aiming point again and shot this same area. Since this was not an area of interest, we just filed these photos away. One of our interns was tasked with cross-referencing these coordinates and came up with the match. We have conclusive proof that this way station has not been active more than three months. I thought you would be interested in these shots."

Carter answered some questions about the possibility of previous shots of the area. There was no record in the files of any development in that area before the past three months. There was no evidence that this could have been an active point that had fallen into disuse and then been resurrected even for different purposes.

Bringle took a much closer look at the photos. By sheer luck, like a needle from a haystack, fate had handed him a history lesson on this tiny piece of real estate. Now it was his responsibility to interpret the lesson. Did this confirm his doubts about Cho Dinh, or did it in fact confirm that he was giving them new and viable information about this activity? Bringle knew he had to make the call.

From this point on, the burden would be his to bear. He had to develop a plan. This was a showstopper if he couldn't provide a strong rationale for the actions he was taking. He was sure that Barstow had received the same briefing from Carter that he had. He assumed that Barstow was giving him time to evaluate the evidence and analyze the mission. Go or no-go? He was feeling the pressure begin to build. He knew the worst thing he could do was to rush into the decision.

As he thought about the times he had been in the field and called upon to decide a course of action, he remembered that more often than not, if someone were leading you away from a particular course of action, that would be friction, sometimes covert or sometimes overt but always that attempt to sway your actions one way or the other. After careful consideration, he came to the conclusion that there had been no pressure for a course of action. All that had happened had been an offer to sell information for dollars. That was the crux of the matter. Dinh did not appear to be trying to work him beyond his obvious desire to fatten his bank account safely hidden away in Switzerland.

Bringle had decided. The mission would continue, if he could persuade Barstow. He made arrangements to see the ADO that afternoon. His trip to the eleventh floor was surprisingly uneventful. Barstow gave no sign of having had any of the briefing knowledge beforehand and was supportive of Bringle's interpretation of the data. If there was any hesitation on his part, he was hiding it well.

Bringle knew the next round of negotiations was coming soon, and his apprehension of all that could go wrong was growing by the hour. He was eating antacid tablets by the fistful. But he was also growing ever more confident of his source. Like so many in his line of work, once sold, all sold. He began to see things from a single perspective, losing the advantage of other views.

When the comfortable executive jet departed from Langley AFB, Bringle was in his accustomed seat. He was making every effort to be as unobtrusive as possible. Since most of the delegation had no idea who he was or that he was anything other than a minor figure from agriculture, it was not difficult to maintain his front. There was not the feeling of excitement building in the mission he had experienced on the last trip to Paris. He felt that he would be apprehensive of his contacts with Dinh from this point.

There was probably a reason that Bringle was having more trouble convincing himself of the reliability of the information being supplied by Dinh than he had of convincing his superiors. They were relying solely on his descriptions of his contacts with the North Vietnamese informant. He was the one trying to read every nuance of every meeting for hidden clues about the man's motivation.

During the initial session at the usual meeting place, Dinh showed no visual sign of recognition of his handler. Once again, during dinner, served late due to French custom, Bringle noticed some of the North's delegation had chosen the same restaurant as he had. Not surprisingly, Dinh was among the diners. Bringle knew better than to attempt any sort of contact.

He was taken by surprise when the waiter arrived at his table with a bottle of champagne. When he looked the way of the Vietnamese delegates, they each raised their own glass to him in an informal toast. Returning the salute, Bringle downed the bubbly. He had to acknowledge they had good taste in champagne. This was really good. Soon, the delegation from Hanoi had finished their meal and was gone. He was disappointed to see Dinh going out the door among them. He thought, *No contact tonight.*

Immediately, he was thinking of the danger the agent might be in. He had to be very careful of any contact with the foreigner. As he sat contemplating the peril in which the other man might have placed himself, he reached for the bucket containing the champagne bottle, thinking to pour himself another drink of the good stuff. Only then did he notice that the label on the bottle had been tampered. There was a loose spot along the upper edge of the label. Examining it more closely, he could barely see the edge of a tiny scrap of paper.

Freeing the paper from the glue of the bottle, he read, "Last freebie 9-15." Carefully, he scooped the scrap of paper up from the table, placing it in the breast pocket of the suit jacket he wore. Then he returned to the main course of his dinner. If anyone were observing, there was no sense in tipping them to the fact that he had been contacted. After a nice cigar, he leisurely returned to his hotel. Once inside the legation, he prepared the message for transmission via the transatlantic cable. Using the security parameters prescribed by agency protocol, he soon had the message encoded. After handing it to the head of communications, he returned to his room. He had the best night of sleep he could remember for a first night out.

The next morning, he took the specially prepared packet of materials to the meeting. After opening remarks, the teams broke up into interest sections for more discussion of the minutiae they were coming to view as the normal course of the negotiations. Approaching the head of the Vietnamese industrial group, he nodded pleasantly. "This is for Mr. Dinh's review." His voice was pleasant, and he hoped it had not given away the tension he always experienced when doing this part of his job. The senior man nodded pleasantly and indicated Mr. Dinh as if he had just arrived from another planet. Bringle quickly handed him the packet with the note inside, acknowledging receipt of the previous evening's note and "100,000 next visit, see you in Geneva at the address" the final part of the message.

Bringle found it extremely difficult to even feign an interest in the talks he was attending the remainder of the session. His mind was racing; he was no longer considering all the options. He had firmly thrown his hat into Mr. Dinh's ring. He knew in his heart that there would be no turning back from this point.

When the session wrapped up, he was early at the counter in the Charles de Gaulle Airport for the departure to Dulles. All the way home, he was presenting his justification to Barstow for $250,000 of agency money. It was easy to wrap his arms around that figure once he had come up with it. It was also, very quickly becoming the agency money as opposed to the money of the US government or the money of his friends and neighbors. This new perspective enabled him to coolly contemplate the actions needed to carry out his amended plan. Mr. Dinh was about to receive his money but not all that was being requisitioned for him from their black operational budget that the agency maintained for such contingencies as this.

He had to come up with a compelling story for Barstow. He figured once he had the ADO on his side, getting the money broken down into manageable proportions would be simple. It would go to several offshore accounts he had opened during the time he was operating in the South during the period of hostilities. No one had ever questioned any of his non-accounting practices nor had he ever been able to explain to his superiors why he was not overjoyed to come to Washington for the conclusion of his career. He had taken a severe pay cut to come to Washington. He had, on more than one occasion, gotten quite a quiet chuckle out of their perception of him as a bumbling idiot.

He had been careful to occasionally nurture that perception from time to time. How could someone teetering on the brink of incompetency have been fleecing everyone with whom they had had contact for over ten years? He had to keep up the façade.

After a period of contemplation, he felt like he had the basis for his tale for Barstow. It took only a short while to come up with a new second note that he had received from Dinh, threatening to expose their agreement if he wasn't immediately compensated an additional sum of $150,000. This, of course, would be routed to the address in Geneva provided in his earlier message. Unless paid, there would be no further information on the way station.

Dinh would never know that the money had come into his account and been forwarded to several Cayman Island accounts within minutes of its arrival. Of course, the Swiss banker who had helped with the transaction had gotten a handsome slice of the proceeds. Barstow had fallen for the ruse and signed the requisition and witnessed the transfer of funds. He had the receipt to prove how well he was spending the money of the people of the United States of America.

Bringle passed the word to Stidham that everything was a go for the mission. Stidham never needed know about the details of the transaction. His team would go to the rendezvous point at Duc Lo and find whatever was there. They were grown men and great soldiers, if they were taken advantage of—well, bad on them. Bringle thought to himself, *I never took them to raise.* With that thought and the balance sheet for his offshore accounts, he felt greatly at peace with the world.

Bringle loved his country. He wanted the best for his country. He was a firm believer that what was best for his country was always what was best for him. Therefore, if it was in his country's best interest for someone to get paid for information, he believed it's best for him to get a slice of that pie.

The second tenet of his core values was that everyone who worked for the government was expendable. So far he had never had to extend that line of reasoning to himself, but he was overly capable of telling himself that this was in fact true. He especially hoped that based on the information he was paying Cho Dinh to produce, Stidham and his men would be able to get some of the American POWs out of the hellhole they were being held in over there.

The fact that he had figured out an angle to benefit his favorite charity in the whole world, Marty Bringle was simply icing on that cake. If the mission cost some of Stidham's men their lives, which he hoped it wouldn't, that was another cost of doing the business of war. He had worked hard at developing his worldview. In the days prior to 401ks and thrift savings plans sponsored by the government, he had perfected the art of skimming enough operational budget money to finance his independent retirement fund safely hidden in a Cayman Islands bank account away from the prying eyes of the IRS. He was quite expert by now in making funds regularly arrive there for his later enjoyment. He had spent almost thirty years developing the techniques and exploiting the banking contacts he had developed in Switzerland and the Caymans. He was sitting on top of the world. He was about to engineer the heroic feat of rescuing these American servicemen or at least getting funding for his plans.

Barstow, on the other hand, had observed Bringle at work for most of the thirty years. He had always felt a bit of reticence toward the field operative, but there had never been enough mud to stick to him over the years to get him into a pot of sufficiently hot water to burn him thoroughly. Therefore, he had been allowed to operate. There was a tenet in the shady agency world that what didn't kill you made you stronger. Bringle had certainly been involved in enough shady deals to have been thoroughly brought to a boil, but it had never happened due to the combination of good fortune and the throwing of others to the wolves, which had been done without regard for those. After all, they were all expendable commodities of the United States government.

With this understanding of how things operated, Barstow reluctantly authorized the payment of the additional $150,000. Bringle had the money wired to the account of Cho Dinh, and with his contact in Switzerland cooperating fully for a small slice of the money, within fifteen minutes, the money had mysteriously disappeared from the Vietnamese government official's private account and reappeared in Bringle's account in the Cayman Islands.

Cho Dinh was, of course, notified of the deposit but was also informed that the transaction had been a mistake and the oversight had been corrected. Since he was not expecting additional monies, he accepted the explanation. Besides, there was another round of peace talks coming up. It was time to bait the American a little more.

The next day, the team reported for training at 0700, after rising early for their PT and personal hygiene. They were soon over at the heavy rigging shop at Campbell Army Air Field. The day's lesson consisted of learning to rig the quarter-ton vehicle for dropping from the C-141 airplane. The morning was spent in the classroom area learning the theory behind the heavy drop, the techniques for the rigging, and the utilization of various techniques for diverse purposes. By the afternoon, they had moved on to a hands-on presentation upon one of the mock-up aircraft deployed around the field. Under the tutelage of the rigger school and the watchful eye of Sergeant First Class Taylor and his minions, the young recruits were soon submitting their work for review. Of the four quarter-ton vehicles prepared one was returned for rerigging. Considering this was their first attempt at this skill set, the instructors thought that was pretty remarkable.

Nuckles, thinking of those men in that POW place, needing those vehicles to get them out, thought that was not acceptable. He soon had the team working in two man teams, and the rigging was brought to standard. That's when he made the decision—tear out all the rigging. When the vehicles were stripped, then he started the two-man teams over. Soon the four quarter-ton vehicles were standing ready for inspection again. This time, there was no doubt. All vehicles were ready to go.

At 2100, the C-141 passed over Bastogne DZ, and the rigged vehicles were plummeting toward Mother Earth. Shortly after, a short stick of ten jumpers joined them on their way down. As the men made their landing approaches, they were relieved to see that they had managed to get close enough to the vehicles that there would not have to be a long march to the rendezvous point. All jumpers and vehicles were found to have successfully negotiated the drop.

Removing the rigging, the team divided into the four vehicles; and by 2230, all were secure and back in the debriefing room. Today's debriefing was much smoother than the previous day's event. When called upon for his comments after getting the feedback from the evaluation team, Nuckles asked, "Sir, would it not seem more feasible to do our drops from the night sky well after nautical twilight, considering the environment we will be encountering?"

Scandretti was ready for this one. "PV2 Nuckles, I think the major is getting ready to add another layer of difficulty to this whole exercise, which will address your concerns about the nighttime jump." That was all he felt at liberty to say, but he was concerned about the stories he had heard from the off-cycle instructor teams about the equipment that had been coming into the possession of the team. He thought he knew what they might be seeing as a new tasking. He was thinking that night that jumping was likely to be a small part of the new modus operandi.

At least for this day, they felt satisfied that they had successfully added an arrow to their quiver. The next day and those to come would determine if that would be sufficient. The pace of the mission was quickening.

On Wednesday, they once again were allowed to sleep in until 0700. They were out of the chow hall and standing in formation at 0830 for what would become a seventy-two-hour day. They received the frag order from First Lieutenant Scandretti and began to devour the mission. They were to perform a reconnaissance in force of an area located fifty-three miles from their present position. They had to be on point NLT forty-eight hours from that moment. Sound, noise, and light discipline were to be enforced throughout. They were to assume they were under constant observation.

They were given two hours to prepare. Nuckles gave the team thirty minutes to pack their rucks. Since these had been done the previous evening, that took only long enough to pick them up and bring them to the assembly area. The team immediately broke the frag order down into manageable bites and began to divide responsibilities. Nuckles made Foster responsible for requesting required peripheral equipment. They received glasses, compasses, map sheets with overlays of expected enemy activities, and suggested routes, and they were given a full OPORDER and OPLAN outlining the situation into which they were being inserted.

Finally, he lined them up and personally inspected each man's gear, spare boots, socks, uniforms, canteens (two per man), rifles, ammo, concussive devices, pyrotechnics (which they had been assigned as a basic load), gas masks, which, at this time, did not have hoods, and the steel pot, which was capable of multiple uses in a field environment. Wiznewski had been tasked with drawing the team's C rations. When he had gone to draw them, he had been informed by Sergeant Gibson that each man would receive three C rations not three days' worth. He was just now getting around to mentioning these fifteen minutes before SP time. In reading the frag order, it was noted that local survival subsistence was authorized.

A quick consultation with Sergeant First Class Taylor determined that this heretofore unheard-of term meant they were authorized to eat whatever they could secure from the land that was edible. This meant that the session on nuts and berries was looking like something they wanted to recall. Nuckles figured that Foster could probably snare a rabbit if they had time to set one.

By the time they had fully packed their rucks, they were each toting about seventy pounds. This would keep them reminded of what they were carrying over the course of the days that they would be on the trail. With a last look around at his team, Nuckles shoved off from the SP and headed down the trail they had preplanned to take for the first portion of the exercise. As he walked along, he thought perhaps he had overreacted to the news of the reduced C rations; after all, he had gone three days occasionally without eating while growing up. He figured that they wouldn't starve, maybe a bit discomfited.

Having arrived at this conclusion, he realized that he had better get to concentrating on the area and the surroundings where he was finding himself located. It seemed as if the route they had been assigned had intentionally been selected to pass them through every marshy, boggy area of the military reservation possible.

After three hours of exertion, he checked their coordinates with the map against the terrain features he saw now. He realized that they were making very good time in spite of the heavy undergrowth of vegetation and the ground conditions they were encountering. They were about three-quarter mile further along than they had laid out to be at this juncture. He decided it was time to call a halt. Sending Foster about a hundred yards ahead to a point with an unimpeded view of anything approaching them, he motioned for Ash to drop back and protect the rear. He and Wiznewski would get the first break.

They had taken a sip from the first canteen and were replacing them in the covers when the sound of something in the underbrush off to their left made them freeze. Immediately, Nuckles thought that the sound was emanating from some OPFOR activity. He began to ease his way toward the sounds. After negotiating through a heavy thicket, he came out on a ledge overlooking the back side of a small lake. Not fifty feet away was his OPFOR activity. A mama black bear was teaching her two cubs to fish, and when they failed a task, the reprimands were swift and resulted in the loud grunts he had been hearing. Relaxing, he spent a few minutes enjoying the sight before moving back to Wiznewski and sending him to relieve Ash and hurrying to the point so that Foster could come in and relax a few moments.

They were soon moving down the trail, again keeping a very brisk pace considering the loads they were carrying. They took special care to make a wide pass of the mama bear; they did not want to be an object lesson for the cubs. After two hours more of humping it down the trail, Nuckles decided it was time for lunch. He knew it was chancy, but he decided to bring everyone together so he could communicate with all for a few moments. He reminded them that they were short on rations. If they ate an entire meal now, they would have nothing left to munch on over the evening. He left the decision to each man as to how much, if anything, was eaten. Shortly, he had established overlooks on the trails ahead and behind while they took their rest. There was relatively little food consumed as they all had an ample breakfast.

As they moved along, Nuckles and Foster found themselves in the center of the march. Quietly, Nuckles slid up to Foster's elbow. "Nobody has shown us anything about deterrent devices, but when we take a break, why don't we rig a trip wire behind us on the path we have come to enhance our security?"

"Seems like it would help us out," mused Foster. "Of course, if we are being aggressed by the off-cycle men of our team, a trip wire flare is not going to fool them. Still, it'd be better to try something than to let them waltz in unannounced."

"I have an idea when we stop for the evening that may help us out a little." Nuckles was deep in thought as he tried to decide how to approach the security issues they would have to deal with during the time they were on the trail.

That evening, they kept moving until 2100 when Nuckles called a halt. Putting out security elements fore and aft, he soon was working on a device he had decided to construct. Taking a piece of string from his ruck, he began to collect C ration cans from the team members that had been emptied of their contents. He then took his P-38 (can opener) from his key ring and punched small perforations in the bottoms of the cans so that the can would slide up on the string. He then tied knots above and below each can to hold it in place and then strung the next can until he had four cans on a piece about twelve inches long. Tying this to a longer section of string, he took his first creation to the point where Ash was watching the rear trail. Working together, they had soon deployed the device and rigged the trip wire to the most likely avenue of approach with the most limited visibility. Having repeated the exercise with Foster at the point, he returned to Wiznewski and lay down to get a couple hours of sleep. They would relieve Foster and Ash at 0001. At 0300, they would hit the trail for the day's activities.

It seemed that his head had barely hit the ground when he was awakened by the banging of something metal on metal out in the woods nearby. Suddenly, he heard a familiar voice using some of the most colorful language he had heard recently. Pausing slightly, it dawned on him that the voice belonged to Sergeant First Class Taylor. He slipped out into the woods to find the senior NCO entangled in the trip wire he and Ash had so diligently placed not so long ago. Ash was holding his M16A1 at the ready and laughing at the man trying to loosen himself and making more noise and getting caught more every time he moved.

"I have him covered," announced Nuckles. "Deadpan."

"Comedy" came back the reply.

"Well, Mr. Comedian, what are you doing tangled up in all this?" Nuckles couldn't help being pleased at catching the senior NCO in his trap.

Taylor had finally given up and relaxed, and the bonds seemed to relax with him. Ash impishly motioned at the contraption. "We used to catch small game in these back home. The more they tense up and struggle, the tighter the cords are pulled. A small improvisation after you went to your rest." By this time, he had set Taylor free.

"Now I assume you came out here for a purpose," Nuckles was addressing the NCO gravely. "I don't imagine you were sleepless wondering how we were faring. What's up?" Nuckles was very much aware that he had the upper hand in this exchange. A cautionary alarm was ringing loudly in his brain as he considered the situation.

"We have had you under surveillance since you left," Taylor offered.

"Must be one fine surveillance plan from what I see of your maneuverability out here," Nuckles shot back.

"Touché," was Taylor's feeble rejoinder. "We wanted to get a closer look at your defense. That was a very good job on the deterrence by the way. I would caution you"—and he pointed at Ash—"when you have an intruder, be careful not to give your position away to him or to others who may be outside the wire and watching."

Turning to Nuckles, he continued, "You did a very good job in coming up unannounced and unnoticed to assist, but again, be careful. With such a small body, you can easily become overextended in this area. A larger force could lurk about and take advantage of the opportunity to isolate you guys from the rest of your party."

A soft chuckle was heard from nearby. "I don't think anyone has been isolated out here, Sergeant First Class Taylor." It was Wiznewski from the cover he had adapted behind the scene of the incursion. Having no need to announce his presence, he had simply maintained good position and was now in command of the situation.

Surprised, Taylor said, "I do believe we have things under control at this time. If I may be excused, I will get on back to my team." With that, he arose from the position he had assumed in the perimeter and began his trek back to the balance of the evaluation team. The three men watched him go until he was out of sight.

"Good work." Both of their efforts had saved the day for the team. Each had scored a big attaboy for their actions in this encounter. Motioning to Ash, he said, "Go on back to base and get a little shut-eye. We'll need to hit the road about 0300." Turning to Wiznewski, he added, "Could you go relieve Foster so he can get a couple hours off his feet also?"

As Wiznewski turned to go, he heard Foster call out, "I'm right back here. When I heard the commotion back there I moved back a little to maintain visual contact with you guys. I couldn't see guarding way up there when there was no one in the middle."

As Nuckles thought this over, he realized that the instinctive move made by Foster had been the best choice. Given the small size of the team, they could have easily been overextended in one direction to the point of losing contact with the forward element. Still, he thought the radios we requested would have really come in handy for this very reason.

At 0255, he quietly slipped into the main position and woke the two resting members of the team. In a few minutes, they were ready to hit the trail. They made certain that they had secured all their belongings and no relics of their visitation of this site remained behind.

As the day progressed, they continued to make good progress. Finally coming to an area of dense vegetation, Nuckles decided that it was time for a break. Maintaining the security of the perimeter, each man was able to get a few minutes of rest. Wiznewski had the point. Motioning to Nuckles, he indicated a large object in the trail ahead.

"What do you make of that?" Nuckles asked.

"Well, if these glasses are good for reading English, I believe this might be someone's C rations." Wiznewski grinned. "We may have found our local subsistence."

Nuckles nodded, thinking he was pretty sure that they were not the intended recipients of the largesse lying in the trail ahead of them, but he had been authorized local subsistence. While he was almost certain that the lieutenant had intended this to mean the killing and cooking of a rabbit, squirrel, snake, or other small game, this had not been expressly forbidden. While these thoughts were going through his mind, Foster arrived at his elbow. "They really nailed us yesterday for lack of initiative." His interjection was enough to satisfy Nuckles.

"We only take enough for us to have two meals today and three tomorrow, including what we already have. No need toting a whole lot, and someone may be looking for these meals in a bit."

They had soon secured a case of the C rations and were on their way. Without incident, they moved down the trail. At the forty-mile mark, they broke for lunch, with confidence now that they had sufficient rations for the exercise. They were finishing their meal, each dispersed and facing out with interlocking fields of fire, when Major Stidham suddenly materialized on the trail. None of them had seen him coming until he appeared. Indicating Nuckles, he motioned for him to come join him on the trail. "How are your rations holding out?" He quizzed the younger man. Nuckles had a premonition that this was not going to be good for his future as the platoon guide.

Honestly, he answered the query, "We have enough for the balance of today and tomorrow."

"Can you explain how you got three meals each and now you have at least four meals per man? Is this related to the loaves and fishes story I have heard about from the Bible?" Stidham was trying hard to get an explanation without accusing anyone of misappropriating government materials.

Nuckles explained that they had come upon the pallet of C rations out in the middle of nowhere, there had been no one around, and they had taken only what they needed. They had an OPORD authorizing local subsistence, so they had taken advantage of what they found locally. Stidham was secretly pleased by the explanation, but he still had to appease a first sergeant some distance back who thought he had a gripe because his unsecured rations had disappeared. VunCanon was a likely candidate to handle this item of sergeant's business.

"Let me assure you that local subsistence does not include any C rations you might happen on along the route." His stern tone indicated he was not buying the explanation he had heard.

"Sir, two days ago, we were raked over the coals for not exercising initiative in regard to items we could have requested for our mission. Today the exercise of that option is getting us in trouble. I don't see a whole lot of difference." Nuckles was earnestly making his case.

"The difference is that the objects day before yesterday were available for a signature. Today's objects were taken with no accountability having been established. We have pretty much given everything anyone has requested for this class, but even we have to account for the resources we use." Stidham emphatically stabbed the air as he talked.

Chastised, Nuckles understood the differentiation. He still wasn't happy, but he had a feeling that the time had come to beg forgiveness and move on. "Sir, I see the error of my ways. If it will make things right, we can give up the case of Cs we took. Each man will still have one meal."

Stidham was not about to volunteer to carry the case of Cs back to the clearing and confront the angry Tennessee National Guard first sergeant he had left VunCanon to deal with. But this did seem a workable solution. Taking the case, he winked at Nuckles. "No man traps today?"

"No, sir, not for a short break" came the response.

With that, Stidham was off and heading back up the trail. When he had negotiated a sufficient distance to be safely out of range of the young team, he carefully stashed the C rations in the crook of a hollow tree and was soon on his way. He had been impressed with the spunk shown by Nuckles in standing up for what he believed to be the right thing. He simply had to be taught what right looked like. Obviously, he had been briefed by Sergeant First Class Taylor on the perimeter defense abilities that were being honed by the members of the team. This had made a big impression on the NCO.

The team gathered around Nuckles after the major had departed the area. "Was he mad that we didn't call at ease for him?" questioned Wiznewski.

"Naw, he just wanted the C rations back." Nuckles was not going to harbor any ill feelings about the lost food. He quickly gave them the thumbnail view of why they could not keep the rations. After a little grumbling, the team seemed to accept the decision. They brightened considerably when informed of the positive comments of their previous evening's endeavors. It was certainly encouraging to be appreciated.

They made quick work of the remaining miles required to be covered and were assuming their overlook positions of a small village resembling one seen frequently in pictures they had seen from Vietnam.

"This is it," Nuckles pronounced as they lowered their profiles onto the ridge overlooking the village. "Everyone knows we are to observe and record. Avoid engagement unless fired upon. Ash and Foster, swing around the back side and try to get a different vantage point. I have a feeling that the big hut in the middle and the larger one on the periphery are the keys. If we could get a look inside them, it might be helpful. Don't expose yourself to discovery, but if it becomes doable and you can look without being seen, do it. Keep a good log, and remember cover and concealment. You should be on station in thirty minutes. Two on and two off during hours of darkness. Don't let your buddy doze off on you. Good luck."

Looking at Wiznewski, he added, "Well, partner, I guess we should get settled in for the long haul. It's starting to grow long shadows. We probably have two hours of visibility at most. You want first or second watch?"

Wiznewski replied, "I didn't sleep much last night. Let me doze." A few minutes later, he was sound asleep.

For the first hour, there was no activity. Then a family of five dressed in Vietnamese costumes came down the street and went into the larger of the buildings. A few minutes later, they were joined by a second group of four who went into the same hut. Eventually, about thirty individuals were moving around from building to building. Occasionally, Nuckles would catch a glimpse inside one of the huts. It looked unremarkable. But every move and observation was dutifully entered on the log they carried for this mission. As the sun sank over the horizon, he realized that he had let Wiznewski get a few extra winks. But now it was time.

He stayed with the awakening young man until he was certain that the grogginess had left him. Then showing him the log, he found his resting spot and was overcome by his exhaustion. It seemed only seconds later he was being shaken awake by Wiznewski.

"Everything okay?" he queried. The young man nodded and then said grimly, "Look at this." Showing Nuckles the log, he pointed out that shortly before sunset, the women and children had disappeared into the huts, and only the mature males had come and gone since then. Nuckles made a brief note on the log to that effect. He was about to declare Wiznewski relieved when a figure emerged from the far end hut and hurried down the street toward them. Along the way, two more dark shadows emerged. They were almost to the edge of the village when it dawned on him. The three were all women! As he watched, the women went a short distance out of the village.

There was no doubt what they did next. They very quickly and efficiently placed a booby trap across the path coming into the village. Once again, he was busy recording events. He had the location that each had come from and then watched to which hut they returned. A small drawing of the location of the device went onto the log.

Things seemed to die down then. The balance of his shift was uneventful. He awoke Wiznewski with much less effort than previously and was beginning to note that his tiredness seemed to have dissipated somewhat. They chatted about their observations for several minutes before he went to his resting spot. He had no doubt that they were on to the saboteurs. When the shifts had resulted in the 0400 shift being Wiznewski, with no activity noticed, they both had begun to think that the villagers had turned in for the night.

Wiznewski was munching on the cake he had saved from his C ration of earlier when he was startled to see just a glimmer of light come from a door on a ninety-degree angle from where the woman had first appeared in the twilight gloom of yesterday. As the shape crept down the street, it was soon joined by another and another. Suddenly, Wiznewski became aware that the shapes were not large enough to be adults. They were children. Only ten to twelve years old, he estimated. Watching them, again, they went outside the village and were busily constructing a device that had every appearance of being a booby trap. Again, it was noted the origin of each individual and to whence they returned.

When it was 0500, the village came alive with activity. There was coming and going internally, but there was no traffic on either path leading from the village. At 0545, Nuckles stirred and was soon peering into the gloom of a dawn that was slowly materializing. As Wiznewski showed him the entry, Nuckles asked about the location of the device. Wiznewski soon had a rough sketch of its location.

As they were finishing this, a commotion was heard on the trail. Coming down the trail in route step was a company of US soldiers. Wiznewski was halfway out of the concealed area they had secreted throughout the night when Nuckles got him stopped.

Wiznewski whispered furiously, "We have to warn them. They are headed for that device the women planted."

Nuckles just as adamantly shook his head. "No our orders are to observe, nothing about interfering. They are in enemy territory marching over uncleared ground. They have to find this. I'll bet our test is to see if we give ourselves away to save them."

"Well, if I knew this was what we were doing, I would be somewhere else. I cannot watch Americans march into a trap." Wiznewski was becoming vehement.

"I'll bet these guys are being tested, similarly to what we are facing." Nuckles voice was calmer than he felt. He hated to have to hold back his comrade, but he was almost certain of what they were facing. He pulled the frag order from his pocket and pointed to the mission statement. "O-B-S-E-R-V-E." He pointed to the word. "No other action verb. We don't have enough information to disobey an order."

Finally, Wiznewski calmed down. When the approaching unit discovered the sabotage and disabled the device, he turned to Nuckles sheepishly. "You're right. I'll be okay now," he whispered.

Nuckles did not respond. He was busily entering the events into the observation log. Soon a second unit approached the village on the second trail. There was a loud popping sound from the second device that the unit managed to locate with their feet as they stepped on the trip wire. This set the observers arguing among themselves again as to whether they had done the right thing. Finally, Nuckles had said, "We'll see when we get our review."

Wiznewski set his jaw. "I could never watch our boys going into an ambush and not warn them. If you can, I don't understand how you rationalize that."

"I'm following a lawful order given to me in no uncertain terms. If intervention was allowed or encouraged, the order would be worded differently. I happen to think words are very important." Nuckles was not backing down, but he was growing weary of the debate.

About thirty minutes later, they were startled by the approach of boot steps behind them. Looking up, they saw Stidham, VunCanon, and the Scandretti's team coming up the ridge. "God job on the observation." Scandretti's comment was directed at both. As they started to question him, he waved his hand. "An excellent topic for the after-action brief. Where is the balance of your team?"

Nuckles grinned. "We thought two angles better than one. They're watching from the other side."

"Well, let's go get them." The lieutenant was already headed straight down the hill. Securing the other team members, Nuckles retrieved their log, which was remarkably similar to the one composed by the first team. Reading it over carefully, Nuckles did note an entry that was off cycle from his own and raised an eyebrow at Foster, "What happened at 0230?"

"I think a dog went through the area. I thought he was going to set off the first trip wire but he turned into the bushes just short of it. I thought we should note it. You probably couldn't see him from your side." Foster was proud that his excursion around the village had paid dividends, even if they were marginal.

They arrived in the village in time to see the two units departing the area. When Scandretti opened the door to the large hut, they could see for the first time that it was laid out to be an operations center for the village. The actions of the villagers were easily controlled and synchronized from there.

Motioning them to their seats, Scandretti took charge. He talked about C rations and asked VunCanon for his input. "It reminded me of something I would have done myself a few years back. But you have to be accountable for what you get." There it was—short and simple. Nuckles started to take the blame when three dissenting voices cut him off, "We all had them on us. You didn't make us take them," they choroused.

The senior members seemed ready to move on, so Nuckles sat down and shut up. Then the mention of field deterrents came up. Scandretti turned to Sergeant First Class Taylor, "Sarge, would you say that they showed ingenuity in developing an early warning system?" He almost got this out with a straight face.

Taylor looked up in mock surprise. "I'm sure I don't know what they have achieved in that area. I was simply out for my evening constitutional when I came upon some strangers in the wood who were kind enough to make sure that I found my way." His whole team was roaring by the time he finished.

"I guess they get a go on that subject, but seriously, that was on the verge of genius, and I want PV2 Ash to show me that knot that he was using when we finish. The idea to tie in the noisemakers with the limited number of claymores you were given was a real innovative approach. We did think that you were perhaps uneven in your perimeter coverage from the instructions we heard being given, but when the breach was attempted, we were impressed with the adjustment you made to a defendable area. Wiznewski, you were exactly where you were needed, whether by design or chance, we do not know, but it worked."

Moving on, he covered the observation of the village. He asked Nuckles to come to the front of the classroom to continue this discussion. "The log you developed was again innovative and a good tool for learning your craft, but we would caution you. On real-world missions, you run the risk of compromising your mission when you start writing down observations. You need to develop the technique to keep them up here." He lightly tapped the side of his head. "Also, if you are observing a real hub, you may not be able to keep up with writing." He added, and then seeing Wiznewski's hand, he acknowledged the question.

"Sir, we were deeply into whether we acted properly by not alerting the unit moving into the area of the traps they were facing. What is the correct doctrinal disposition of this?"

Scandretti looked at Stidham and grinned. "That's why they pay majors the big bucks, sir?"

Stidham glanced around the room. "I want everyone here to understand that when you are given an explicit order, you follow it explicitly. Failure to do so indicates lack of discipline. There can be no debate, discussion, or question about this. Do I make myself clear?"

"Yes, sir" came the echo from around the room. Even the seasoned soldiers felt compelled to respond to this direct question. There was no doubt in anyone's mind about what the standard would be in this unit.

Stidham looked around the room. "We will be moving into a new phase of our operation starting now. We are going to be practicing HALO jumps for the next few weeks. We will make one jump here to get our feet wet, and then we will have several practice jumps at different places around the country. If all goes well, we probably have a month before D-Day for our live mission. I wanted to let all of you know how proud and pleased I am with the products we have turned out here. Congratulations to you guys for accomplishing so much in this time. However, this is not the end of your training. We are simply transitioning to a new phase."

Stidham looked over at First Sergeant VunCanon and noted that he was already on his feet. With a half grin, he asked, "Anything to add, First sergeant?"

VunCanon called the young men they had been working so hard to bring up to their standards to the front of the room. "It is a proud day for the unit when young men receive their jump wings, and you have already achieved those. It is an altogether different and proud accomplishment to receive your ranger tabs for your shoulders. In country, we were never very formal about these matters, but since we are establishing precedence here, why don't we make it a nice one from the start?"

With that, he had each man remove his fatigue blouse and he handed him a replacement that had been altered with the Second Ranger Battalion unit patch and the ranger tab over the unit patch. Upon completion of handing out the new blouses, he paused for a moment. "I don't usually make long winded speeches. Those are normally made by men who don't get to talk at home very much, but I want to take a minute and tell not only the four of you, but also"—and he turned to include the entire room of soldiers present—"you have all made me feel like a proud parent these past weeks as you have grown and developed. The trainees obviously have grown from the taskings they have faced, but the trainers I have had the opportunity to see have developed their abilities to train and mentor the men under their tutelage. These men have developed their training tactics and provided challenges, which have allowed them and the trainees to grow even more. I say thanks to each of you."

Sergeant First Class Taylor was the first to reach Nuckles but by no means the only one. All four of the new rangers were soon enveloped in a wall of well-wishers who were wearing out the backs of the new fatigue jackets they had just received. It seemed that every one of the team wanted to personally congratulate each man. It seemed natural that, shortly, the ceremony had moved to the NCO Club, where it would continue with toasts and speeches from all.

The four new men were the first to feel out of place when they realized where they had been taken. Foster looked at Nuckles and gave him the sign; they soon had excused themselves from the group and were headed to the latrines. "This is not the place for us." Foster bemoaned as he entered the latrine doors. "It could have been worse. They could have taken us to the O Club." Nuckles shot back at him with a chuckle.

"But we can't come to this place on our own recognizance." Foster was in a dark mood. "We should have our celebration somewhere we can at least get back into if we decide to come back some day."

"Point well taken," Nuckles observed as they completed the washup that accompanied the trip. "But do you think any of these guys has anything but our best interest at heart by doing it here? And by the way, I don't think it's just our celebration. If you think about it they have an accomplishment to celebrate also, they have turned out their first class."

Foster considered this for a few moments and then grinned. "I guess my ego was getting out there for a second. Thanks for getting me back in line. I'll be fine now." With that, they went back to the party, from which they had hardly been missed.

Week 5

Dallas 13–Minnesota 15
Baltimore 29–New York Jets 22

VunCanon was at the door of the operations room when he heard Stidham call his name. He quickly turned and went into the commander's office. "Yes, sir," he reported with a touch of formality that was usually not evident in his bearing. Stidham noticed and raised an eyebrow in a questioning manner.

Slightly embarrassed, the senior NCO stammered, "Sir, I was on the way to the juniors' barracks to bring them up to speed on the mission." He was trying mightily to keep from sounding judgmental, but it was obvious something had gotten under his bonnet.

Stidham asked, "Do you feel that the idea of keeping them apart from the team structure is not working?"

"Sir, it was my idea to put them under you and I. It's just causing me to have to remember to update them after I update the NCOICs like I do with Gibson. I simply have to adjust my strategy."

"Would it make it easier to institute a lead member of their team?" Stidham asked.

"Maybe for communication purposes, it would save me having to find all of them every time to put something out, it would be one and done, and then he could tell the others." The first sergeant thought about this solution and realized that Foster had been a PFC a week longer than the other three. "Since Foster is slightly senior to the others, we could make him the lead member of the group."

"When you go over there, handle it." Stidham had settled that problem. "Is there anything else on your mind?"

"I think I simply have a case of pregame jitters, sir." VunCanon was way too old to have these doubts.

The reply caused Stidham to smile. "Top, when you have the jitters, I'm thinking there's some little detail that I've overlooked or forgotten. You know I trust your judgment. I need you to be my eyes and ears on this." Stidham was as matter of fact as if he had told a kid to take the dog outside, but he knew he had to get the first sergeant to realize how much he depended on him for his leadership, not only for the formal lines with the NCOs but also with the informal things he could accomplish with the junior officers of the team.

VunCanon finally looked him in the eye and said, "Permission to speak bluntly, sir?"

"Granted." Stidham showed no hesitation. Whatever was on the first shirt's mind was on his too. He wanted focused leadership from his team.

"Sir, I know we recruited these guys with the mission in mind, but this is turning into something none of us has ever done before. We are learning with every move ourselves. Is it really fair to these guys to subject them to such an experience? We took on the task of training them, sir, and right now they are learning from the experience, not from the trainers." VunCanon had never put into words what he was thinking, but Stidham had seen the same metamorphosis taking place with the young men.

"Top, you know I immensely respect you and your opinion. But I have to say that the young men are in on this now. They are learning on the fly, but think back to Vietnam. Didn't we all learn on the fly over there. Even in the second and third trips, we were still learning. This is a lifetime exercise in our business. I really appreciate that you have made these young men into your soldiers. Quite honestly, I was afraid that just the opposite might happen, that there would be resistance to having these young guys in such a crucial stage of a very important mission. Thanks for not letting that happen."

"Thank you, sir, for setting me straight," VunCanon mumbled. "I guess I better go see Mr. Foster, senior PFC." They both laughed as the top shirt picked up his hat and headed for the door. He was quickly off to the barracks.

Foster and the others were sitting in the open bay of their quarters, discussing their perspective of the day's training, when the first sergeant came into the room.

Wiznewski was first to see the visitor and called, "At ease."

"As you were" was the response from VunCanon. "I wanted a minute with you guys, if I might."

They all chuckled, knowing full well that he might. Their time was his time. He could have all of it he wanted. He quickly filled them in on the decision to identify Foster as the lead team member and that all communication to them from the leadership of the team would come through Foster. They would still operate as a group when performing the mission tasks. Then he filled them in on the mission for the next day.

As all soldiers will tell you, never decline a chance to sleep late even though it probably means no sleep the next night. After all, they could have had you work all day and then pull the night duty. You'll lose out on enough of these in your career, so take advantage when one goes your way.

They were immensely interested to find that the quarter-ton vehicles would be part of the exercise tomorrow evening. They were somewhat concerned that they had not had any practice at dropping them previously. Now they would get their first opportunity to exercise these additional skills they had acquired. But they were young and quickly adjusted fire.

When they were told that the reporting time for tomorrow would be 1300 at the pack shed, there were smiles all around. Then Foster thought about what lay in store for them and asked the first sergeant, "I know you told us 1300, but with getting the vehicles ready for drop, could we come at 1130? And by the way, can the motor pool be open for us about thirty minutes before that?"

VunCanon remembered the days when he had been young and for a moment envied them their enthusiasm. Then he thought about the mission they would soon be undertaking and snapped back to reality. "We'll get the motor pool open, and the keys will be ready. Just bring the vehicles over when motor stables are complete. Remember, no oil leaks. We don't want to GI a C-141 for dropping a few drips of fluid in it." They all took note of the reminder that every detail was of importance, and the first sergeant left.

Nuckles watched the back of the first shirt go through the door. Then he turned to Foster. "Congratulations, buddy, senior PFC is all right."

Each man quickly added his thoughts of congratulatory nature. Soon the mood in the room returned to semi-seriousness. They were making plans for getting the vehicles over to the pack shed for heavy rigging. They had had some experience doing the rigging for low-level jumps with static line openings, but this was a little different.

Ash pulled out his ever-present notebook and referred to the pages he had devoted to the previous few days. "Here it is," he finally proclaimed. "I had picked the brains of the youngest team member from the experts who have been with us. I figured that sooner or later, we were going to get an opportunity to jump these bad boys."

They were all soon engrossed in reading the differences and additions necessary to prepare the vehicles for this special drop. There would be a second chance, but none of them wanted to be the reason that Major Stidham had to go request new equipment from his bosses. Besides, they had become attached to these vehicles. They had all given names to their special chariot.

At 1130 the next day, all thirty-two team members were gathered in the pack shed even though they were not scheduled to be there until 1330. They were all a little apprehensive about the new jump techniques they were becoming accustomed to exercising and particularly the doing of it at night. The seasoned veterans who had served in the Vietnam theatre previously knew that the day had always belonged to the US forces, the Army of the Republic of Vietnam (ARVN), and their allies, while the nights were owned by the Viet Cong (VC) and North Vietnamese Army (NVA). This had an unsettling effect upon them as they realized the balance of power might be shifting ever so slightly.

With these thoughts in mind, each of the team elements were concentrating on getting their equipment squared away for the evening's drop. They were not that conscious of the arrival of the new team members until they noticed that the quarter-ton vehicles were being prepped for their air delivery. As they took note of the workmanlike attitude of the younger troops, they had to give them a grudging amount of respect for the work ethic they were displaying. They had all been impressed with their class performance up until now, but this side of things you never knew about until the test under fire came. They had certainly gotten off on the right foot.

Slowly, individual members of the other elements began to drop by the work stations where the quarter tons were being prepared. Seeing something needing to be done, they would pitch in and lend a hand. Soon the vehicles were rigged and waiting for loading. The fuel load was checked carefully. They would not take more than a quarter of a tank and one five-gallon can of fuel to reduce the chance of a mishap destroying the vehicle upon termination of the drop.

Soon the younger guys were preparing their personal gear just as the experienced team members had been doing upon their early arrival. The older guys were, of course, assisting them in making sure that the correct preparations were being made. Clothes were checked for no tags or identifying marks. Everything was subdued or black. Identification tags that they had been drilled to never leave behind were left behind. All such items had been placed in lockers for storage when the owners would hopefully recover them upon completion of the mission.

Foster looked around as he completed his personal gear preparation. He had been very subdued throughout the evening and the early part of the day. He was not sure why he had been selected to be the lead member of the element other than the fact that he had been in the army a week longer than the other three. Still, he was determined to do a good job at what he had been asked to accomplish. But perhaps even more, he was afraid of failure. This fear would drive him to double and triple check every detail. He began to know that fear was not a crippler of ability but an enhancer that drove you to accomplish tasks that you didn't think you could do.

Stidham had stayed in the background throughout the pack shed preparation phase of the mission. Even though he had told his troops to report at 1330, he, like all the rest, had been there by 1130. Actually, he had been there at 0800; but they had no need for that information, so he didn't share it with them.

Having observed the interaction of the younger team members with the more experienced members that had taken place so far, he suspected that integration of team functions was about to become much more easy and thorough within all facets of the team. He had been hoping for this since day 1. He called VunCanon over and pointed out what he was seeing and sensing. VunCanon tried to deflect the credit to the team NCOICs, but Stidham was adamant. "I know what you were up to last night, and I don't know how you pulled it off, but I suspect there may have been other meetings over an adult beverage after you left the team area yesterday evening. Thanks for what you have accomplished in getting the team organized and pulling together in the same direction."

This praise was something that VunCanon was not accustomed to hearing nor had he sought it. He was simply doing his job as an NCO. In his mind, every

NCO in the army would have eventually done the same thing he had done. Some would have done it faster and some slower, but all would have seen what needed doing and gotten it done. That was all he had done, according to his thinking.

Stidham, for his part from this moment on, would never think of his team as split between trainers and trainees again. From this time on, they were all simply team members. There were no longer any divisions other than the team elements that each had a unique set of objectives to accomplish if the team mission was to be a success. He was equally confident that if this required assistance from element to element, it would be forthcoming without hesitation. They had indeed become a team.

Week 6

Dallas 27–Kansas City 16
Baltimore 27–Boston 3

Stidham was engaged in running the training of the school, but he was also busily laying on training and making plans for the preparation of Operation Duc Lo 70. He not only had to think of allied training, but there were a terrific number of resource allocations to be arranged. He did have the advantage of the black budget he had managed to get from Bringle. Still, allocations had to be made and resource timing arranged.

With his usual thoroughness, he soon had reservations for use of the Vietnamese mock-up villages that had been constructed on every military post in the Continental United States (CONUS). He had guessed at the timing using the time-honored Scientific Wild-Ass Guess (SWAG) method, and he had inflated the number of days to give him a little wriggle room. He had laid on support from the USAF for flights, which the CONUS bound plans and operations sections were happy to have because of the restrictions being placed on real-life missions. He found it ironic that during this time of budget cutting, they were turning him loose with a blank check book, so to speak.

He had also spoken to a contact he had made in CINCPAC during his days in Vietnam. He had tentatively arranged for a submarine to be patrolling just off the coast of North Vietnam, but the exact dates had not been arranged. This had cost him big-time in the nonfinancial collateral accounts that were often more important in the military than the actual budget numbers.

He had accomplished all of this and still kept the training pace for his school and his teams at a get-ready-for-action pace. His four-man school had done its first four jumps and was ready for the fifth. He would accompany them for the big event. These young men had completed CBT, equivalent AIT (MOS training), and now they were ready to finish jump school, all in the past four weeks. He was really proud of the selections they had made for the school candidates even when he remembered the difficulty they had encountered in getting the candidates aboard.

As proud as he was of the school candidates, he was equally proud of the twenty-eight men who were serving as the cadre for the school even while breaking into teams to prepare for the mission that so far they knew only as "the mission." They did know that it had the potential for danger and that they would need to be at their best to have any hope of pulling it off. They were becoming masters at getting into the compound at the infiltration range and neutralizing the guards in the facility. Each team took pride in getting into the compound and getting out without the guards being alerted. The guards, of course, had the advantage of home field and knowing roughly the schedule. Still, the practice sessions were running about fifty-fifty on success.

The team leaders were being stretched to keep the competitiveness under control and avoid physical contacts between the teams that could result in friction between teams. They had done an excellent job of arranging events that would rely on cooperation between teams and coordinated efforts shortly after any head-to-head events were carried off. So far, these efforts had paid huge dividends. Stidham was particularly proud of how these junior officers were working out together. He could see evidence of their bonding every time he watched an event.

As he joined the jump candidates for their run to the packing shed, Stidham felt that things were going well for the team. If the team was doing well, then he was also. Each man was all business as they went about the serious matter of packing the chutes they would depend on for lengthening their descent. Stidham had no time for observing, as he was equally engaged in preparations for the coming jump. It was just as serious to him as it was to them. The intensity with which a jump was approached did not lessen with experience; it was a matter to keep one out of a grave for all involved.

As they left the pack shed and headed for the green ramp, the air became much lighter. The banter between the men was lighthearted but tinged with concern. They seemed to know that sometimes even men who were experienced jumpers might come up with cold feet. They had promised one another a helpful push if it appeared there might be a situation developing. Ash playfully turned to the major, "Sir, do we need to include you in the pact?" His query was not abrasive, and the major grinned.

They were not aware that he had debriefed the flight crew from the previous jump and that he was very much aware of the events of yesterday. However, if the men had let it pass, so would he.

"I don't believe you will be there to see if I have to be pushed since I'll be the last man in the stick." His reply touched off another round of teasing among the men. They soon arrived at the green ramp, where they received their last safety briefing and were soon boarding the plane. The jump order had been set. Wiznewski would go first and then Nuckles followed by Ash and Foster and then would come the major. That would complete the stick for the school. Unknown to the students, the entire staff of the school would be jumping with them. They would have a ceremony for the new certified parachutists after the jump. Team spirit was being built here. As often occurs when the army rents a plane from the air force, there were a number of other jumpers who were trying to get a seat on the plane to keep their jump status current, so the C-141 was soon filled to capacity. There would be several additional sticks of jumpers after the school jump.

Stidham had recently been studying the best way to insert his troops. He had been aware of High-altitude, low-opening techniques, which had been worked on for years. The problems with that had been oxygen deprivation, nitrogen in the blood stream causing a high form of the bends, failure of the individual to open the chute at the prescribed time, and exposure to extreme cold at the altitudes common to the technique. Although experimental jumps had been made from much higher, he had come up with the idea of jumping from around thirty-one thousand feet.

Overcoming the problems he had encountered required some ingenuity. He had been in touch with Letterkenny Army Depot, home of the storage facility for the army's extreme cold weather gear. He had been able to requisition forty sets of cold weather suits. When they came in to the unit, PV2 Cansler was there to sign for them. When he let Sergeant Gibson know of their arrival, he got a blank stare. "I didn't order them" was Gibson's response. Looking at the shipping label, there was the newly assigned DODAAC code for the school.

As Stidham came in from his morning PT adventure, he heard the two men discussing what and who could this be. Coming around the corner into the common area of the team facility, he saw the four large crates that the equipment had arrived inside. "Have you checked it out? Is it all there, and is it in good shape?" Stidham's excitement was noticeable.

"Sir, the shipping document calls for four cases. I haven't checked the packing slip for backorders since I don't know what is in there. I have no way of knowing what shape it is in." Sergeant Gibson had resumed the status of the NCO responsible for supplies. He was pretty sure he was about to learn what the contents of the crate were, but he would not allow Cansler to take the heat if something were not right. "We can open it up right now, sir, if you have time and want to see whatever it is."

"That is a terrific idea." Stidham was like a little kid with a new toy. Gibson soon had his tools, and the crates yielded their secrets. Gibson could not help looking perplexed. "Sir, I spent a year over there and never put on a field jacket, much less felt any need for any of this stuff. Is there something we need to know about our destination?" His inquiry was phrased to avoid showing any signs of irritation over being left out of the requisition loop, but it did convey a sense of concern over what he may be learning about the team's mission.

Stidham suddenly asked him, "Can you get me a deuce and a half and a team to load these crates?"

Gibson looked at him as if he had lost all sense of reality. "Sir, are you going to send them back?" He was wondering what planet the major had escaped from that morning.

"Just get a deuce and a half over here, ASAP." That was the only reply from the senior officer. In the meantime, Stidham was on the phone to the packing shed. After completing that call, he summoned Sergeant Gibson. "We have thirty-two parachutes on hold for us at the pack house, and can you take care of the hand receipt for them?" He made sure to include his supply sergeant in the requisition process this time. He knew he had screwed the pooch the first time by leaving him out of the process; he would not have it happen again.

When the two-and-a-half-ton truck arrived, Gibson was waiting with his detail. Known as the deuce and a half, these trucks have been a staple of the army since Henry Ford was a teenager. They quickly loaded the crates into the rear of the truck. The young specialist 4 driving the truck looked at Sergeant Gibson and asked, "Where do I deliver this stuff?"

Stidham came out of the building in time to hear the inquiry. "I need you pick up thirty-two parachutes at the pack shed and then follow me. I will show you where to deliver them." Stidham was not ready to brief the newest twist to his mission, and besides, he had several more pieces of equipment to be accounted into the unit property. He asked Gibson to ride with him on the short hop to the pack shed.

On the way to the pack shed, he had time to alert the supply sergeant to the impending arrival of the additional items. Some would be arriving by different means, but they all should be coming during the next two days. When they had secured the parachutes, he had Gibson accompany him, while the detail rode in the back of the deuce and a half. They soon reached their destination—the post quartermaster laundry facility. Off-loading onto the receiving dock was soon complete. The men were looking around, wondering what was going on, but none of them were going to quiz the major. He, for his part, had asked that Gibson keep mum about the newest equipment of which they were becoming owners.

Their perplexity grew to new heights when the supervisor of the facility came out to the major and inquired, "Is this the equipment you want us to prepare? Will there be any more to add to the dye lot?"

"I think this is all," Stidham replied and then reached into the crate that had the top loosened earlier. Pulling out a pair of Mickey Mouse boots, he observed, "This pair is black, but I think you may find some are white. Can you find some dye that will color any of those?"

"I think we have exactly what you want." The supervisor made a quick note on the hand receipt Gibson was handing him. These should be done by tomorrow, after 1600.

With that, Stidham thanked the detail for their efforts, and the truck roared off to return the men to the facility, while Stidham and Gibson went to the operations center at Campbell Army Airfield. Going into the facility, Stidham was soon explaining what he needed to the chief of operations. He was requesting 40 individual handheld altimeters and 160 pressure opening devices. Again, the chief had exactly what they needed. They were soon on their way.

Gibson still didn't know exactly what was happening, but he did know that his document register for the supply room was growing some real meat on its bones today.

When they arrived back at the unit, they found a second shipment had come in, and PV2 Cansler had again signed for the materiel. "Sir, I don't know, but this may be intended for the hospital, but the driver insisted it was to come to your attention. I don't know why we would be getting oxygen bottles."

Stidham and Gibson were struggling to get in the door when Cansler finished his tale. Laughing, Stidham winked at him and asked, "Is Top in his office?"

"Yes, sir." As the major handed him the box he had carried, Cansler realized that he had not gotten an answer or any kind of explanation for the strange arrivals in their building that day. Since the major seemed in a good mood, he took this for a good sign and let it go.

Knocking on the first sergeant's door, Stidham looked around. "Top, can you schedule a team meeting this afternoon after the team training is complete? We have some new developments, and I would like to cover them with the team today. If you have time, I would like to bring you up to speed on all this over lunch. My treat."

VunCanon grinned and allowed responded, "Well, the pres wanted me to come over, but I think I can shove him back to 1400 since it's you."

Stidham laughed out loud, glanced at his watch, and said, "Ouch, the time has flown. Ready to go?"

They were soon on their way. Stidham mentioned the HALO jump concept, and VunCanon acknowledged that he had heard of the practice but had no experience, knowledge, or great interest in the technique.

"Does this have something to do with the strange shipments we have been receiving today?" was his first response.

Stidham explained that he had been researching the technique and had found the problems outlined above. Some had suggested pressurized suits for the cold and the nitrogen/oxygen problems, but that did not seem practical for their application. So he was looking at giving each man an oxygen bottle, an altimeter, using the extreme cold weather uniforms that had arrived that morning. Use of the oxygen bottles would require that the men go through a lean air breathing exercise for at least forty-five minutes before taking off. He thought that with the slow ascent of the C-141, his men would not have trouble with this issue, but it was too easy to fix to take a chance. He went on to explain that the cold weather uniforms were being dyed black and the labels and all identification insignia being removed even as they spoke. He mentioned picking up the altimeters and the pressure opening devices from the operations team at the airfield.

After a while, VunCanon looked over soberly and said softly, "I do believe the stuff is about to hit the fan. Would we be jumping wearing black for any particular reason, sir?"

Grimly, the major looked him in the eye. "Nighttime operations seem to go better if they can't see you coming down."

"That's about what I thought you were telling me." The older man dropped deep into thought. He had no further comment, electing to keep his thoughts private. The waiter came and took their order. They were soon reflecting over Weiner schnitzel, which was the special of the day. VunCanon finished his main course and, when the waiter approached with an inquiry about dessert, observed that he probably should have a piece of the pecan pie, but he really wasn't up to it today. The major also passed and received the bill, and after paying, they were soon on their way back to the unit.

"You seem pensive," Stidham observed as they drove along the main street of the post.

"Well, sir, I guess this is not going to be such a simple snatch-and-grab if all this is necessary to get in there." This was the reply from his senior enlisted man.

"Top, I don't want to scare anyone, but I believe we take every precaution to get in there without anyone noticing. Take care of our business and get out of Dodge. We don't want to take out an advertisement in the *Hanoi Times* that we are coming." Stidham was earnest in his response. VunCanon was reassured that every precaution was being exercised to safely execute their mission.

At 1800, the common area had again been transformed into a secure briefing area. The team gathered around the room, making small talk until the entrance of the commander. Paying the correct military courtesy they were quickly engaged in the briefing.

Stidham went through very quickly—the shipments arriving to the unit that day, the purpose for the materials they had received, the trip to the quartermaster laundry, and the reason for that exercise. He was sure that the detail of men who had carried out that portion of the day's activities had probably filled in their counterparts as to what they had been doing. Now he had the chance to remove the rumor part of the equation and begin to flesh out the story. After hearing the story of the development of the HALO technique, the men were enthusiastic.

Staff Sergeant Evans raised his hand and was called on by Stidham. "Sir, are you saying that we would be the first to pull this off in combat?" he asked.

"I'm not sure. There are rumors that MACV-SOG (Military Assistance Command-Special Operations Group) may have done something like this at some point already, although apparently for a different purpose. You know, with the classification rules, we don't get all the details." Stidham spoke quietly, but his words had the reassuring effect he had hoped to achieve.

"Well, I'll be." First Lieutenant Scandretti spoke up from the front row. "I always wanted to marry that little girl in the black dress at my high school homecoming dance. Now I get to be the one in black."

By the Monday morning, after the long controlled exercise for the school participants, Stidham had arranged for an expert team from Ft. Bragg to come assess both his plans for the drop and his techniques for getting the team into position for the drop. When he showed them the equipment that had been appropriated, they were impressed with the quality of research and the technical savvy that had been brought to the concept of the mission they were preparing to evaluate.

The men from Ft. Bragg who had been instrumental in the development of the techniques for the HALO and for assessing which equipment would be essential in the implementation of the process realized they were dealing with a professional group of soldiers. Getting their attention to the details would not be a problem. When they reviewed the equipment, none of them remarked at the blacked out labels or lack of information in the garments. They had dealt with black operations enough to know not to point out the obvious or to point out the precautions being taken. They were, of course, glad that they could provide their expertise to the planning but not their bulk to the performance of the mission.

Stidham was dealing with a slippery issue. He had to give enough details to the team of experts to allow them to function, but he had to carefully assess their need to know anything of the details of the proposed mission to avoid possible compromises or divulging of information. After all, he had no way of knowing who was watching the watchers he had brought in to watch his team.

The HALO experts were professional at knowing that there were topics they could know about but at the same time maintaining the veneer of invisibility that they would pretend to not see those things that they could not divulge to anyone else. Of course, the detailed mission brief they had received upon their arrival had also prepared them for this venture into legitimate paranoia.

As soon as possible, Stidham had the men from both teams assembled in the common area, which, of course, had been prepared for the high security required for the mission essential elements that were about to be spoken of by the team members.

Stidham thanked the visitors for coming and for their innovative approach to developing the craft of warfare from aboveground level. He had no need to mention the shoulders of the men they stood on as they prepared to take the next step to a higher understanding of their position in the grand scheme of things.

They, in response, were appreciative of the willingness of these men to attempt to accomplish something that had not been done. But to be honest, every one of the people in that room were genuinely concerned about the effects that this technique could have on freeing from cruel punishment men who were being held in less-than-ideal conditions by a brutalizing force intent on keeping them in that condition.

As Stidham went through the brief, he touched only on the need to deploy secretly into enemy territory and the consequences of early detection of that insertion and the intent of the uses to be made of that insertion. It came as no surprise that the decision came down to a night drop on the blackest night of the month leading up to the operation.

After careful consideration of the options available for the operation, Stidham turned the meeting over to his four team leaders, with instructions to have a fleshed out proposal of the operation by 1200. While the visiting experts were not engaged, he took them off to the side and began to pick their brains for the fine points of HALO operations that may have eluded him to this point.

The team chief looked over the controlled chaos engulfing the common area and said, "Sir, this is some leadership style. I don't believe I have ever seen anyone encourage pandemonium as a planning tool for military operations."

Stidham coolly nodded and answered, "While I agree this looks rather undisciplined, wait and see what their proposals look like. I bet they won't be far from what I had originally laid out myself, but now they will be their plans so they will take ownership of the effort. What I really need from you guys is the key differences for preparation of the jump, HALO versus a standard opening jump that we normally perform."

"Well, obviously getting the men on an enriched-oxygen breathing routine is one of the first things, but it starts with the pack preparations. We have a standard chute preparation guide set up for these situations. You have to ensure that each man has an altimeter working, that his pressure opening device is correctly placed and ready to function. I think in this particular event the preparation of the uniforms is even more critical than usual. You have made a good first step there in getting the cold weather gear from Letterkenny, but don't forget fit and functioning of each piece of gear. The smallest piece of equipment can become essential if it fails to function properly or doesn't fit the user correctly."

"Well, I asked." Stidham was not upset at the laundry list he had heard. It was almost identical to the research he had conducted himself. What it did was corroborate his efforts and also provided him with updates on the newest and greatest devices. He wanted his guests to feel appreciated, but he did not intend, for one second, to turn any facet of the operation over to any outside experts if he could avoid doing so. A secondary benefit of this exchange was to engrain on the members of his team the importance of each item being added to their package.

By the time the teams were completing their proposals, Stidham was ready and waiting for them. He and VunCanon took the primary seats, while the visitors and the four new trainees filled the balance of the room. Each team was called one by one to present their version of the mission to the command group.

As each team presented their thoughts, they were seated, and the following team came into the room. Before seating the teams, VunCanon would have them outline their proposals on a sheet of butcher paper. The sheets were then hung on the wall backward until all teams had presented. While the team members were seated, they were not allowed to make changes to their proposed plans. Stidham pointed out that this was not to teach them to be inflexible, but it would be better to work on all the plans than continuously try to improve the first.

As each presentation was made, it was impressed on Stidham how much his team respected one another. Several times, when points were being discussed, he heard murmurs of "I wish I had thought of that," or "Man, I forgot about that as a factor. I knew we had to consider that." These comments told him the team was not just giving lip service to what they thought he wanted in the plan, but they were genuinely involved in arriving at the details of the plan.

As the four young men who had recently become team members sat and listened, it dawned upon Stidham that he had not specifically included them in the plan preparation phase of the operation. Subsequently, on several occasions, he had spoken out about an issue, but rather than say how he wanted it handled, he would ask one of the new men for a recommendation.

This assured him that they were not sitting through the briefing half (or more) asleep and that they felt included in the development of the plan. By 1400, the team presentations were complete. The teams broke for midday chow at the closest dining facility and were back in the briefing room by 1500.

When they arrived, they saw that the command group had been very busy. The butcher blocks had been turned face outward and the differing points highlighted in the new yellow marker that was the current craze.

Stidham took the podium. He quickly went over the variations of the plan. As he had predicted to the guests earlier, he could have used the basic presentation from any one of the four teams and made few corrections or additions to them. Yet he found elements in all four to specifically include in the final plan. The young team members were impressed that he allowed so much self-determination in the structuring of the mission. The visitors were amazed that out of the near chaos they had witnessed earlier, they were seeing the completion of a plan incorporating their specialty (The HALO jump) into what would obviously be a major development in the war.

Stidham had carefully avoided the introduction of any discussion of the actual mission, concentrating instead upon the critical factors of this new jump procedure. He knew that his men would have reservations, but if he told them it was necessary for the completion of the mission, he had no doubt that they would "Lead the Way."

By 1730, they had a very much working plan for their first orientation flight the next day. The visitors had been called on to tweak the plan and had made a couple of valuable suggestions that this team had not anticipated due to its inexperience in this field. They were most favorably impressed that there were no objections of "it can't be done" or "we never did it that way before."

Stidham shortly gave the word to break up the meeting, and the men moved out to accomplish their individual routines for the day. As everyone was exiting the briefing, Stidham asked the head of the visiting team for a moment. "Chief," he began, "one thing I'm not real comfortable with, the pre-mission oxygen enrichment seems to me to possibly call for an extreme amount of oxygen bottles to be transported. With the logistics of what we are doing and the preparation for it, I'm not so much worried over the cost. You and I both know the government will waste much more money than that while we do what we do. But I am concerned about getting enough aboard the plane for the mission and having enough logistically at each of the practice sites we will be conducting."

"Sir, have you considered the air force as the source? They have drop-down oxygen masks at each seat on the plane. If the men went on the oxygen provided when they got on the plane, by the time takeoff and preflight activities were performed, they would have over thirty minutes, and they could actually stay on the oxygen until they were ready to move to the ramps."

Stidham thought about this for a while and decided he was glad he had brought this guy in to address the problem. He had gotten a workable, fixable solution to a thorny problem from it.

The following day, at 0700, the men were lined up at the pack shed, ready for their first lesson in preparing parachutes to open from pressure devices as opposed to rip cords attached to the plane or manually activated during a jump. They had soon mastered the technique of inserting the pressure sensitive device into the chute cover and were ready to move to the green ramp.

Arriving at the green ramp, they were quickly shuffled off to the waiting C-141 cargo plane sitting at the terminal. They had been briefed and were not expecting an instantaneous takeoff when they shuffled aboard. Finding their seats, each man applied the oxygen mask to his face per the instructions in the device. The team leaders quickly checked each man to assure that the devices were functioning properly and that they were applied in the proper manner. Then they sat back and enjoyed the ride.

By the time the flight pre-operations checks were complete, they had been on the oxygen for twenty-eight minutes. As they pushed back from the gate and trundled down the taxiway to the takeoff point, Stidham noticed the time. He was looking at VunCanon and nodding at his watch when he felt the thrust of the engines as the big plane lurched forward and down the runway. In a few seconds, they were airborne.

He sat back to relax during the short flight to the drop zone. But his ever-active mind was far from shutting down while he was at ease. He was going over in his mind the package delivery of the quarter-ton vehicles and what would be the best delivery method for their use in the mission. Looking over at VunCanon, he noticed that the older man was certainly not carrying the relaxation thing too far out either. Noticing his commander looking at him, he gave a weak grin. "I never can fully trust these flyboys all the way. I always get a little nervous," he confessed.

"Well, let me take your mind off the nervousness part," Stidham lightheartedly jabbed at him. "Have you given any thought to how best to deliver the quarter-ton vehicles during the mission? As I see it, we have the option to deploy them first, mix them in with the jumpers, or to hold them until last. There seem to be advantages to any of the options, but there are also drawbacks to each."

Stidham paused, hoping the top sergeant would jump into the conversation. "Well, I think at first blush that we don't want them coming down into the same LZ we are using after we are on the ground." VunCanon paused now to give his commander the reaction time to head him off if he was going down the wrong rabbit trail here. Hearing no clue that he should halt, he continued, "I believe that mixing them in creates is a potential safety problem with the chutes getting tangled possibly. So, sir, I guess my recommendation is that they go first but not by much. We want to be landing about the time they quit bobbing up and down from the shock of hitting the ground. It'd be even better if their area of the LZ could be isolated slightly so there would be no possibility of a man hitting one of them while landing." VunCanon sat back in his seat, exhausted from saying so much all at once.

Stidham nodded, patted him on the shoulder, and said, "Thanks, I know I can always count on you for good feedback. That means a lot."

Presently, they were aware of the plane making slight adjustments to the flight path as the pilot lined up the LZ for his approach. Soon the Christmas lights went on at the head of the ramp. The jumpmaster, standing by the rear cargo ramp, looked like a character from a science fiction movie, with his oxygen assistance package and the safety straps to ensure that he didn't become part of the jump package. The team members were fairly sure that he was not about to voluntarily come join them on the first drop.

As they departed the plane, the first impression was that they were hurtling at ever-increasing speed toward the hardness of the beautiful earth stretching out endlessly below them. Even though the team leaders had been through the gaining of terminal velocity and they were aware that they would soon achieve that speed, they still had not expected TV to be so fast.

Watching the altimeter he carried with him, Stidham soon noted that he was approaching six thousand feet, which had been set as the preordained opening altitude. Sure enough as the altimeter indicated the arrival at that height, Stidham felt the jolt of the chute as he was yanked up to the heavens by the opening. He had not been fully prepared for the shock of the opening, but it was not something to be feared, just respected.

He was soon noticing little puffs of clouds above him; they had chosen to use the standard white chutes today rather than the especially black-dyed chutes he had ordered to be prepared by the quartermaster laundry. They would get plenty of practice with the "black beauties," as the men had immediately dubbed them. His team was slowing from their descent and preparing for their return to Mother Earth, from which they had so recently departed.

Upon seeing the beginning of the chute deployment, Stidham soon realized that he had better begin to look for a landing spot, while he still had some maneuverability and altitude with which to work. He noted a suitable landing spot and was soon lined up on it as he traversed the final twenty feet. Landing with a thump, he quickly set about recovering his chute. Quickly restoring it to its carrier, he was already studying the terrain and giving instructions for the securing of the operational area that his team now owned.

As VunCanon and the team leaders made contact with the ground, they similarly began to assume the mission posture required for them to transition from a group of passengers aboard an air force flight into a highly functioning military fighting force responsible for this piece of real estate. They were well into the securing of the area by the time the last set of boots hit the ground.

As the area was transformed into a site for the performance of a finely tuned outfit, the men began to perform the tasks they had trained so arduously for since their arrival at this post. Few words were spoken, and often, the ones that were spoken were redundant. The troops were so organized and motivated to get the area under control. Each man realized the criticality of his piece of the pie for the overall mission. In addition to this, redundancy was built into every task so that if someone were unable to perform his tasks upon arrival, there was someone else already performing it, just putting on a little extra mustard.

Everyone was soon in position at or around the rally point (RP) that had been assigned them as the mission was planned. All reports were handled by the responsible parties, and the perimeter was under close scrutiny from the team members assigned as the security force. The four newest team members had been assigned to help the team medics since the quarter-ton trucks they would be responsible for operating were not part of the team mission today. They were engaged in an evaluation of previous POW releases in other wars, trying to evaluate the severity and type of injuries they were likely to encounter in this group of POWs they hoped to be bringing home in the next few weeks.

The medics had been studying everything they could get their hands on from World War II and Korea. They had studied the POWs held in the Pacific during World War II especially closely. They were really becoming concerned about the state of mind of the prisoners with whom they might have to deal.

Stidham, checking in on them during the exercise, had overheard some of the conversations. "Don't get hung up on the emotional and psycho things, for two reasons," he counseled. "First, they will not have been held for an extremely long time. These things won't have had time to do deep-seated damage yet. Second, you won't have them for a long period either. We will be handing them off to professionals trained to deal with the things they are dealing with, and you won't get the bonding time to develop the extent of any psycho/emotional issues they may be experiencing. We primarily need to be able to adapt to any physical things they bring with them."

Reassured to a certain point the medics were soon reengaged in their studies. They were dedicated to caring for their fellow soldiers even when they had never seen them before. These men would bear a large degree of responsibility for getting the POWs out of country once they were freed. Stidham was heartened to see how engrossed they were in preparing themselves for the mission.

Shortly, the team was called together, and the event post-brief was conducted. The lead element was the visitors from Ft. Bragg with their evaluation of the HALO. They had to admit that the HALO had been pulled off smoothly for men with no background in these affairs. They had made some minor tweaks to the onboard portions of the pre-jump period, pointing out the importance of the switch to bottled oxygen from the onboard source should be accomplished before the donning of the cold weather gear, particularly the gloves and facial coverings, to ensure no exposed skin to the wind and extreme cold at thirty thousand plus feet and reasserted the necessity of each man being alert throughout the jump as to how the altimeter and pressure devices were interrelated.

Stidham had covered a few points involved with the security of the area. He was concerned about the time required to establish the perimeter and the difficulty of establishing security with such a small detail of men. Sergeant First Class Taylor had brought up the devices he had experienced the young members of the team improvising recently during their schoolhouse training. This, of course, brought on a round of good-natured ribbing; but again, Stidham was impressed that one of his senior team members had spotted an innovative idea from one of the younger members and was wholeheartedly endorsing it as a solution at least partially to a real-world situation they had to solve.

Wrapping up the post-op briefing, he turned the men over to VunCanon, and they were soon loaded on cattle cars and deposited back at the pack shed. Moving into the pack area, they soon had their chutes laid out and repacked for another jump. They were about to wrap this activity for the day when Stidham came in and instructed VunCanon to pull out the black chutes that had been prepared for them earlier. The men were soon preparing a second set of chutes, which were appropriately labeled and stored in the facilities of the pack shed.

Stidham had not given any precise order as to which set of chutes would be utilized next, but the men had gotten the idea that the pressure had just been ratcheted up a notch. They were gaining the insight of their leader, and right now they were reading that things were getting interesting. They just didn't understand the extent to which that was happening. They were about to get the message.

"Tomorrow morning same bat station, same bat channel," Stidham intoned as they broke up.

"Sir, when will we know which chute package to carry tomorrow?" First Lieutenant Abramson inquired. "I would like to be certain we have ample time to evaluate each package." The last was added hurriedly, as he did not wish to sound petulant over having to wait for a decision.

Stidham considered the situation and finally relaxed. "We will go with the standard chute packages in the morning. But make a point to inspect both packs and segregate them for your team. Sergeant Gibson, have you collected the canisters used this morning?"

"Yes, sir." Gibson was relieved to report that his work was accomplished. "I have an appointment at the hospital to get them recharged. They have not been able to do a pre-op evaluation of what the dropout rate will be for our canisters," he quickly added, "but we will have some idea if we run into issues with recharging these canisters, sir."

Stidham looked at him and nodded once again, thankful for this young man's knack of anticipating what needed doing and being one step ahead of the curve in getting those things done. He didn't know from what source he was getting his inspiration, but he was certainly happy that it was being provided.

As Ash, Wiznewski, Nuckles, and Foster moved out of the area, Sergeant First Class McCord addressed them, "Are you young men planning to work out this afternoon?" This was more than an idle inquiry; it was more of an order issued under cover of a suggestion.

Foster quickly responded, "Sergeant First Class, we were thinking of going to the gym and play some round ball. Would you care to join us?" Then thinking quickly, he added, "Or any of the rest of you who care to participate?"

Looking around the area, he quickly noticed no takers on the offer. They had moved out of the area when Captain (P) Jamison whispered to McCord, "Pretty slick for young'uns. Declined your suggestion that they go work out with us and made it look like we are the old fuddie-duds who are too old to play ball at the gym."

"Sir, I just didn't want them to forget to keep training at something every day, especially on days with no prescribed workout regimen." McCord answered back, kind of grumpily, and then added, "But I do see your point. These guys are pretty good for babes."

In the meantime, Gibson had gathered the canisters, loaded them into the 5/4-ton truck he had had drawn from the TMP (transportation motor pool), and was pulling into the hospital area. He found the entrance he needed, delivered his items, and was about to leave when he remembered the balance of his tasking.

"When will I know if there are any problems with the recharging of the canisters?" His question stopped the young man who had taken possession of the cylinders.

"I guess tomorrow when you pick them up. You probably should talk to my supervisor." The mumbled reply came back in a manner that left him wondering if he had asked the right person.

"Can I talk to your supervisor now?" Gibson was wondering how hard this had to be.

"No, she has gone for the day. She will be here tomorrow." There was the ever-helpful worker providing all he could. With that, he turned went through the swinging doors and disappeared. Gibson was pretty certain that his work here was done for that day at the least.

As the youngest of the team moved out, Ash looked at Foster and mused, "I might be glad not to be in your shoes the next time McCord is in charge of PT. There may be a bit of payback coming your way."

"Nah," Foster deadpanned, "the first-class sergeant and I are tight like this." He made the universal sign of intertwining his first two fingers on his right hand and showed it to Ash.

Wiznewski just shook his head and slowly drawled, "Well, if I were a betting man, my money would be on the first-class sergeant."

"Do you guys want to play or not?" Foster shoved the two in the back, and they were soon entering the post gym.

They played two-on-two to games of twenty-one three times. None of them were any great shakes at the game, but the competition was spirited, and each game took over thirty minutes to complete. By the time they had played three games, they were winded. "All the cardio advantages of a six-mile run." Foster allowed as they moved out to their barracks area.

They were soon showered and sitting around their bunks. Nuckles pensively looked at the others. "I think we are getting real close to moving on this." His allowance drew guffaws from the other three.

Wiznewski lightheartedly jabbed, "You mean you think that after the sterling performances we have demonstrated on all these tasks, they would still send us out on a real-world mission?" He got almost to the end of his diatribe before breaking into hearty laughter.

The nodding from the other two said they were all aware that the stakes were being increased at each phase of their training, but they were still content to play a minor role in the ongoing saga that was becoming their life. They soon drifted off into their own little worlds with their own thoughts. They were content for the leaders of their team to take care of the heavy lifting of planning and preparation of their team's involvement in the mission that was coming. They would each be ready to contribute as required and allowed.

The next morning, the team was back at the pack shed where the four junior officers, along with their NCOICs, were inspecting each man's packed materials. As the black equipment was brought out and inspected, they certified it as ready and returned it to the lockers. The standard stuff was carried out by the team members, and they were quickly moved to the green ramp area.

The team members noted that the experts were with them again today for this jump. They would be interspersed with the team jumpers, enabling them to better critique the team performance through the jump phase. It was understood that once they were on the ground, the experts' role had expired. They knew and understood that their role was to be an extra set of eyes and ears for the commander during the phase of the operation they were read into and to remain out of the action once the team was on the ground. What happened after that was not their concern.

They were soon aboard the C-141, which had taxied to a stop and was waiting for them to board. They were pleased to note that the oxygen devices had already been deployed from the overhead compartments where they normally resided. As each man took his device and put it into action, they were pretty much alone with their thoughts.

Team 7, as assigned, attached, and augmented, was developing its own personality. While it was developing, it had not done so to the extent that the outcome was a for certain lock. There was still time for mutations to take hold. Stidham knew that this was a critical time for the unison of his team.

As the big plane taxied into takeoff position, he thought, *We have to get it right today. Tomorrow will come soon enough. Every day we need to progress toward a seamless performance.* He felt the coldness of the oxygen cylinder strapped to the small of his back, under the chute pack and thought, *It just does its job. Doesn't care about the other things going on. That's what we have to achieve if we are going to pull this off.*

As the plane slowly thundered up to its cruising altitude of thirty-three thousand feet today, he felt a quick wave of apprehension as he wondered, *Have I covered all the bases?*

Looking at VunCanon, he noticed the top sergeant was making contact with each man, reassuring them that all was going well. He hoped that the man's confidence and trust was not misplaced. Glancing at his watch, he noted that they had been on oxygen enrichment for thirty-five minutes and, at that moment, saw the jump status indicator lights become lit. *Showtime had come*, he thought and shuffled to the door where he would be in position 1.

Soon he was experiencing the euphoria of free fall as he quickly neared terminal velocity and realized that he had better concentrate, or he and his equipment would become extremely damaged. Passing through thirteen thousand feet, he realized that, if necessary, there was now sufficient atmospheric oxygen to support his demand for survival. However, they had agreed that as long as the canister would hold out, they would stay on the enriched air source. His chute opened flawlessly at six thousand feet, exactly as he had programmed it to do. He was soon on the ground and in position to evaluate the arrival of the balance of his team. His confidence had indeed been well placed in the equipment and in his team. He breathed a sigh of relief.

As VunCanon came down in the trail position, he could enjoy the vista of the chutes popping open below him. It looked like the air force had outdone themselves; every chute was headed for open terrain. Linking up at the RP should be a piece of cake. Then he was on the ground, and he was responsible for his piece of that cake. It was time to get busy.

Every team member was performing their functions except that, once again, the quarter-ton vehicles had not been part of this exercise. So once again, the vehicle operators were tasked with assisting the team medics in preparing for their operation upon arrival at Duc Lo. They had actually had some manikins placed throughout the LZ with simulated injuries approximating some of what they could expect to encounter in a real-life situation. They were all busy and engrossed by the developing situations they were encountering.

Also, on this iteration of the scenario, Stidham had arranged to have a light force of OPFOR (opposing forces) scattered about the LZ. This force consisted of only a four-man team, but it was enough to drive home the point that even one man in the right spot could spell considerable consternation for the team when they deployed for real. This added realism to the exercise would help keep the team sharp and ready to spot troublesome issues before there were live on-the-ground crises.

As the men moved smoothly to the RP, they encountered the OPFOR elements one by one and neutralized them, taking two into custody and terminally ending the career of two individuals. This led to what-do-we-do-with-captives scenarios from the two capturing elements. It was quickly decided that at least temporarily, one of the quarter-ton operators would be detailed to the duty of providing security for these persons. Further decisions would rely on the after-action portion of the exercise for total disposition of these individuals.

Wiznewski was selected to maintain control of the two captured OPFOR members. He arrived at the vicinity of the RP with the two men under guard and very much under control. He had taken one boot from each and made them march across the LZ to his present location with one bare foot and one booted foot with no shoelace in it. He stopped them well short of the RP and sat them in such a manner that they could not observe the RP as they waited for the order to move on to the next phase 1LT Abramson, whose element had taken one of the prisoners, noted Wiznewski's approach and reported it to VunCanon, who was responsible for organizing the ground security aspect of the mission.

Stidham was secretly pleased with the improved performance from the previous operation and the adaptation the team had made to the newly introduced elements of the mission. He had plenty of notes to go over in the AAR. The visitors from the other Home of the Airborne facility in the CONUS (Continental United States) were well pleased by the adaptations the men had made to the HALO approach to jumping. It really didn't matter what they thought, as their time with the team was expiring. By tomorrow, they would have reported back to their home base and moved on to bigger and better things in the minds of those who made such decisions.

During the AAR, it was decided that any prisoners captured during the initial phase of mission would be closely guarded by the quarter-ton operators. They would be relieved of this responsibility when they were needed for transporting released individuals if they were all needed for this duty. Since there was a chance that there might be some redundancy in this point of the mission, it might not be necessary to release all vehicles and drivers. If it were necessary for all to go forward, then some team members would be detailed from each element to release them for their part of the operation.

It was decided that no prejudice would be exercised against an individual attempting to surrender even in enemy territory. Every effort would be made to control such individuals, but extreme caution would be the rule to protect operational security (OPSEC) during the pursuit of the unit's goals. Stidham knew that not all of his soldiers had the same respect for the lives of those individuals they might encounter in this environment. He sincerely felt his obligation to develop ROE (rules of engagement) and RUF (rules on the use of force) to carry out his concept of the mission within the boundaries of the Geneva Convention and, more importantly, within the bounds of his conscience.

Abramson brought up the actions of Wiznewski for an attaboy. Stidham listened to the report of him bringing in the prisoners. He concurred with the attaboy for the innovative idea of not bringing them into the RP area where the ability to watch the operation unfold may have compromised the mission or individual parts of it at the least. He did have to point out that the boot-and-lace trick probably would be ineffective on the ground in the real world due to the amount of time the soldiers of the other side often spent out in the boonies operating with bare feet in any circumstances.

He was favorably impressed with the faculties of the younger team members to reflect upon a situation and make a common sense decision even with no command or doctrinal guidance. He secretly wondered how many much more experienced soldiers would have seen that situation developing and made allowances for the sensitivity of the area of operations if it hadn't been spelled out for them in an OPORDER, OPPLAN, or unit SOP (standard operating procedure).

As the AAR was breaking up, Captain (P) Jamison asked, "Sir, do we need to prepare for a jump tomorrow? If so, which set of gear?"

"Leaders, give me ten minutes," Stidham growled.

As the other team members filed out, he was pulling out the pre-positioned paperwork that Cansler was becoming such a whiz at preparing. Quickly taking note of who had received a copy, he passed out the OPORD for the next day's activities.

"I would like to point out a few of the high spots," he began. "First, you will note late day activities first formation at 1300. Give the men time to get a haircut and such personal matters. Second, we will be jumping tomorrow at 2000. As you know, nautical twilight occurs around here at about 1915. It should be good and dark by 2000. Third, we will be rigging the quarter tons for drop activities with us. Gibson, if you would take a little care with the new guys, watch over their shoulders, but don't do it for them. Fourth, issue any required nighttime-use gear. Fifth, we will use the black gear. All jumps from now on will be in black, for now each soldier carries all ID and tags. Any questions?"

There was a low roar as the element leaders broke up to digest this new OPORDER. While it came as no surprise, they had not necessarily been expecting the ramping up of the operation this quickly. After all, this was the hurry-up-and-wait army they were serving.

Sergeant First Class Goldman looked at First Lieutenant Abramson and chuckled. "Well, sir, I guess we will see if we can hit all these marks in the dark."

Abramson responded, "Sergeant First Class, we can hit them in our sleep. But just to make certain, make sure everyone does their sleeping tonight. I would like the men to have finished in the chow hall and be at the pack shed by 1130 tomorrow. I think we can use the head start on the official report time. Maybe identify any flaws we haven't found yet."

"Yes, sir," replied Goldman. "You never know what little gremlins are hiding in that pack shed." He knew perfectly well there were no gremlins in the pack shed, but he also knew that an actual exercise would force design flaws out into the open. This applied equally to plans and equipment. They had the luxury at least at this point of having numerous dress rehearsals for the operation. But each of them knew that once the first of these rehearsals was in the books, they were subject to receiving the hot call at any moment. They would do their utmost to be ready, but they were hoping to hone their skills by applying their training opportunities.

At 1700, the preparations had progressed to the point that minute details were being checked for the fifth time. Stidham sent the team to the chow hall for the evening meal. He asked them to reassemble at the pack shed at 1830. He wanted a few minutes to talk to his team from a commander's viewpoint, but he wanted their undivided attention. This would give the pre-mission tension a little time to dissipate and hopefully keep their concentration on what he had to tell them.

When the team reassembled, he had them come into the conference room of the pack shed. Standing in front of them, he was humbled. Here he had assembled the very best of the warriors he had served with through three tours in country, and not a single one had declined to serve with him or express the slightest hesitation about being there. There were also the young men who had come into the team through the training route. They had not known for what purpose they were being gathered. They still had no full understanding of it, but they were here, and he had doubt of the reliability that they had found being handed them by these warriors who had dedicated their efforts to training them in how to soldier.

As he began to speak, his voice was low. The men were straining to hear his words. "Men, I am proud of every one of you. It is an honor to serve with such a fine group of soldiers. Today we are embarking on a mission that hopefully will result in some fine soldiers coming home from a POW camp in North Vietnam. There is an element of danger to you. There is the possibility that these men we are going to get will not have to suffer in that camp anymore. I want you to look at these pictures of the holding areas they are being held inside. I think nothing more need be said about the necessity to get them out." He handed to VunCanon the pictures he had selected that best depicted the tiny cages the POWs were routinely held inside.

As the photos made their way around the room, there were comments that "wow, we didn't know this was what we were after." Several names were suggested for the security members of the opposition, and a general atmosphere of animosity pervaded the room. Finally, Captain (P) Mizell stood up, looked at Stidham, and, in a calm but emphatic voice, said, "Sir, lead the way. We are in your footsteps."

Stidham knew he had accomplished the impressing of the gravity of the mission they would be undertaking. There would be no slacking off from these guys during the training time left to them. These POWs were too precious for that too be allowed.

With that, they moved the meeting out into the pack shed's general common area, where they were soon retrieving their personal gear and making certain that the quarter tons and stowed gear were being moved to the green ramp loading area. The grim resolve that they would need to pull off the mission was sitting heavily upon their shoulders, as each man asked himself, "What can I do better to ensure that we get this done?"

By 2000, they were finding their rear-facing seats and preparing to go flying backward. The oxygen masks had been deployed from the aircraft's receptacles, and they were beginning to take in the forced air they needed for their own protection. VunCanon noted that the four medics had taken it on themselves to sit alongside the quarter-ton operators, which made sense as their efforts on the mission would be so entwined. He made a mental note to point them out during the after-action brief they would be doing. They were Sergeant Patterson, Sergeant

Flanagan, Sergeant Humboldt, and Sergeant Van Heusen. These men had really seen the light and were doing their best to integrate the young troops into the operation. Their cooperation would be essential to getting any POWs set free out of the environment they had been held in for some time.

The loadmaster for the C-141 had come by to check on the lashings on the quarter tons for the third time as the flight was heading down the taxiway to the hold area where the final preflight checks would be performed by the crew of the aircraft.

Nuckles, from behind the mask he was wearing, looked at Foster and gave him the thumbs-up signal they had used between them for what seemed like a long time. Owing to their youth, it was a larger percentage of their lives than they realized. They both reached out to Wiznewski and Ash and gave the same signal. They were rewarded with the return signal shortly. They were all feeling better about the mission, especially since some of the gray areas were beginning to be filled in from their perspectives. They were positioned so that they and the four medics would be the first out the ramp after the quarter tons. They would have the maximum time to acquire their equipment and get moving to the RP upon landing. As they went out the ramps, they were rewarded by the bubble behind the aircraft. This phenomenon made the individual fall free of the aircraft, and then he was pulled up to the level that it appeared that he was walking on air behind the plane. The loadmaster had indeed made pictures of several of them as they reappeared in his sight.

The pressure devices on the quarter tons had been set to activate the chutes at four thousand feet, two thousand lower than the chutes the men were wearing. This would ensure the heavy vehicles were on the ground before the troops began to land. Since all would be falling at terminal velocity, there would be no passing while dropping through the air. They now had to avoid the vehicles on the ground, and they would be free to begin their mission. It sounded simple if you said it fast enough.

Soon enough, the chutes were popping free of the packs, the men were yanked up as they encountered the resistance of the open chute, and they began to anxiously scan the dark landscape for clues as to their whereabouts. There were precious few of these, for the LZ selected had been blacked out as thoroughly as was possible by the range control party and the Pathfinders contingent who had been happy to get a jump in and help organize the LZ. Even if they were fulfilling a nontraditional function for their part of the operation, these guys were professional at their work. They would normally have set the area for the landing as opposed to their mission today of eliminating any ambient light sources from the ground area.

Once this mission was fulfilled, they were pulled out of the area to avoid any confusion as to who was actually on the ground in the LZ. They were cheerfully on their way to their barracks by the time the ranger team was approaching the LZ from above. They would be a luxury the team would not enjoy when deployed, so Stidham would not allow them to be part of the play for practice. He believed that you train as you fight and fight as you train. He knew they would still be fighting when hell froze over.

The first to land was Wiznewski. He immediately set about securing his chute and once done began to search for the four quarter-ton vehicles. They were only about 150 yards to the front of where the first personnel had alighted. Moving to them, the four vehicle operators quickly began to remove the materials that had ensured the safe landing of the equipment. Just as they had been instructed, they refrained from starting the vehicle motors until twenty minutes before the scheduled arrival at the RP. During this interval, they were busily scouting out the path to the RP and checking in with First Sergeant VunCanon to let him know that all personnel were accounted for and capable of physically performing their functions. They then returned to clearing any obstacles to their path to the RP. While this was not a huge showstopper in an LZ in CONUS, they knew that when they landed for real near some really bad guys, this would assume a great deal of importance. They also knew that when the time came to move the vehicles, they had to start as one and move as one. There had to be stringent noise and light discipline observed.

As the other team members arrived in the LZ, the congestion in the area increased. They had not really counted on being in such a confined space, but here they were. The team was functioning, and all was proceeding according to the plan. The area was secured, and the men moved to the designated RP ahead of schedule. VunCanon sent word to the quarter-ton operators to move thirty minutes earlier than originally ordered. They were happy to oblige.

At 0300, the team began to move from the RP to the designated start point (SP), where the actual movement to contact would commence. This move was carried out without a hitch. The quarter tons were left at the RP to avoid the engine noise giving the NVA any advance warning of their presence in the area.

At 0400, the lead element (Mizell's team), which had to circle 180 degrees around the area depicted as Duc Lo for the play, moved out. At 0415, the second element (Abramson's team) and the third element (Thurman's team) both moved. They went at the same time since both had to traverse only 90 degrees of Duc Lo. At 0430, the fourth element (Scandretti's team), which had the most direct route to the objective, moved out.

VunCanon, Stidham, and Gibson, making up the command and control party, were close behind the fourth element. All elements were equipped with PRC-77s (radios) sufficient for close ground communications between teams. Using assigned brevity codes and the current communications and electronics operating instructions (CEOI), they reported their positions and readiness for operations as they came into the proper relationship with the objective. They had all arrived and reported early. At 0530, Stidham gave the command, and they moved toward the objective, keeping their firing lanes open and the restrictions to prevent them from firing into one another in mind as they moved. In a matter of moments, they were in the compound. They had compromised the OPFOR dummies and were reporting their readiness. Stidham quickly gave the order for the quarter tons to come forward. Within five minutes, the vehicles with the medics aboard were in the compound where the team had discovered six POWs in the compound. As a medic evaluated each POW, they were assigned to a vehicle, and the vehicles, when full, departed the area for the intermediate objective today known as the final objective, where the recent POWs would be transferred to rubber life rafts and taken to the waiting submarine for transport to wherever the navy had orders to take them.

The latter portion of the exercise had not been put into the scenario as yet because there was not a large enough body of water available here to accomplish this. This task would be practiced during the iteration of the exercise scheduled for Ft. Devens and the final dress rehearsal in Guam. If the mission had been successfully completed to this point, it would not be hard to accomplish these tasks was the thinking that the leadership had engaged.

During the after-action briefing, the team had thoroughly gone over the portion of the landing and movement to the RP. VunCanon noted that they had not actually gotten rid of the cold weather gear they had worn during the jump to protect them from the extreme cold of the upper atmosphere. Even though they would not be doing this during the dress rehearsals, he felt that something should be inserted to give the institutional memory that it was critical on the live mission to get that done expeditiously. Stidham soon had a detail working on it and the problem addressed. Mobile lockers were improvised to hold the uniform items until re-storage was accomplished with all the equipment.

Additionally, there was a considerable discussion about the physical location of the team medics. While it was understood that the primary concern was to get them to evaluate the status of the released POWs, it was also important that they be available if there were injuries to team members during the movement to the objective. Sergeant Flanagan proposed that one medic would accompany a team, Mizell's team, who had the greater exposure during the movement, and that a second medic join with the command and control element, leaving two medics to accompany the quarter tons.

If there were no injuries, these two would rejoin the quarter-ton operators when they came into the compound. After discussion, it was decided that Flanagan would accompany Mizell's team, and Humboldt would move to the command and control element. Thus, Patterson and Van Heusen would be accompanying the quarter tons.

As the team moved to the cattle car for the trip back to the unit area, Stidham asked VunCanon to accompany the quarter-ton operators to take their vehicles to the assigned motor pool. He had realized that none of them had the ability to get through the locks on the gates at this time of the morning.

As the cattle car pulled into the unit area to drop the balance of the team, Stidham recognized a familiar figure sitting in the lone visitor's parking place in front of the buildings. He moved over to see what had brought Bringle to town. He was somewhat surprised at the state of agitation being displayed by the agency man.

Bringle reached for his hand, and Stidham noticed a sheaf of papers. "What have you brought us?" The question was formal and all-business; Stidham had been up all night and had other things on his mind.

"Well, I seem to recall telling you that I had made arrangements for Johnny Cash, the Statler Brothers, and the Carter Family to do a show for your team before you left. They will be performing tonight at the post theater. Have your men there at 1800. These are their backstage passes."

Stidham was taken aback. He had actually forgotten that Bringle had mentioned knowing someone who could make a performance of some note happen. He certainly did not remember setting a date for the event. However, pausing to reflect on it, he decided to relax. The performers were either here or on their way apparently, and he knew the vast majority of his troops were country music fans. If this was the most damage Bringle would do on this visit, he would make the accommodation to the schedule.

Stidham was shocked. "Did you tell them where we are going? How much is being put out? You know that these performers always want their pictures made with the people they are benefitting. I am sure that the men would like to see the show, but I don't know about all this." He paused to let his objections gel, but before he could begin to harden them, Bringle was in the next square.

"All they know is that you are a specialty team and that you will be deploying soon. They do not know the destination. We will invite several hundred men from the post to the performance, but your guys will be able to visit backstage if they desire. There will not be photo ops for either side. Johnny is a little nervous about letting it be known that he is doing benefits. He's afraid the requests will flood his operation." There he had answered every objection, even if not thoroughly, at least in some detail. Bringle seemed to have no concept of the problem publicity could be.

It wasn't that Stidham objected to the performance. He was aware that there would be demands from the media as to why this group was being singled out for such treatment, complicated by the fact that the local Ft. Campbell newspaper would want to ask some questions; and in his mind, they were possibly more dangerous than the national media. He had no doubt that the NVA belonged to a clipping service, and if even a hint of whom the team members were escaped, they could make some incredible deductions.

Worst of all for him and his men, he had not come close to loosening the facts about the botched payment from Bringle. This was due in part to several factors. Bringle had not yet discovered the flaw in his plan, so the performance of the team had come too soon. Also, there was no assurance that the plan would be compromised by the appearance of the celebrities, so Bringle had not gone into damage-control mode. Finally, Stidham did not fully understand the worldview of Bringle—that they were all expendable—so he was not worried about their health. After all, he had provided everything they had asked for in training and in resources for the mission. Anything more was incomprehensible to him.

"Do you think you can have the team ready and on station by these dates?" Bringle was ready to move beyond the concert and make certain they were on target for the timing of their departure. "How is the orientation training coming for the new fellows?" He queried, feigning interest in their development. Stidham knew the real question was can we make them believable as the saviors of any POWs we get out of that place.

Stidham quickly brought him up to speed on their accomplishments to date, and the short-term training goals they had established. He had indeed decreed that this week would be the final period when there would be separate training for the new soon-to-be rangers and the cadre of the school. They would begin that day with escape and evasion followed by observation of details on Tuesday. Wednesday would be devoted to personal and equipment camouflage and concealment, and finally, on Friday, they would study how their operations could be used to the best psychological advantage against their opponent and also for their compatriots.

Having given the thumbnail overview of these training events and objectives, Stidham was quick to add, "Of course, stay as long as you like, and join in the training if you feel like it." This, of course, translated to Bringle as "Why don't you get out of our hair."

Be that as it may, Bringle was not quite ready to leave. He felt the need to review the overall plan for the intervening weeks. Stidham informed him of the coordination he had already accomplished in getting permission to jump into Ft. Pickett, Ft. Dix, and Ft. Devens. He had arranged with the 143rd UAAF Wing for support from dedicated C-141s to be assigned to the operation. Bringle hit on the idea of having a dedicated crew fly all of their missions. Stidham objected that if weather became an issue, the flight crew might not have available hours of operation after standing by for an extended period. He was able to carry the day on this topic.

Bringle was impressed with the forward-looking aspect of the plan. While not every contingency was covered, there wasn't much left out. He felt that the right man had been selected for the job. By 1500, he was heading for Nashville and the return flight to Dulles International Airport.

The team elements were soon busily securing their equipment for the next iteration of the project. No matter who was giving a performance, nothing would be as important as them getting the mission down to a smooth and polished exercise. The various element NCOICs were already ramrodding the cleanup. About forty-five minutes after the main body of the team, the other men had arrived. The troops with VunCanon came back from the motor pool. They quickly joined in completing the securing of the personal equipment, and everything was in its place for the next event.

Stidham had VunCanon assembled the team in the common area and informed the men of the coming event that evening. He handed the men their passes and backstage credentials that would give them access to the stars of the evening. Stidham was about to introduce Bringle and acknowledge his role in bringing about the evening's entertainment when he noticed the agency man going out the front door. In a few moments, they heard the start of the engine and saw him through the door as he drove away.

Stidham sent the troops to their quarters with instructions to get some rest and be back at 1730. They would be going to the theater in a group. He wanted to emphasize to them how much team membership meant and how hard they had worked to build that team. He knew they would not take it for granted that they were a team nor would they forget those men who composed that team.

Stidham was soon sitting in the parking lot of the base BOQ (bachelor officer quarters) where he saw Bringle's rented car standing. Moving to the lobby, he asked for Bringle's room and was soon knocking on the door.

"You left in kind of a hurry." He began to speak to his acquaintance. "The men were really appreciative of the passes and the entertainment. Most of them are country music fans."

"Yeah, well, I have other things to do. I was getting packed." The agency man brusquely moved about the room, securing the few possessions he had unpacked during his stay.

"Well, I thought you would want to know we will be jumping into Ft. Pickett next week to hone our skills on a new set of objectives." Stidham was trying to advance a peace offering, but he had the feeling that something was definitely wrong with the agency man. He knew that Bringle had always struggled to feel an accepted part of anything he had worked upon with the man. Now he was offering that acceptance, and he seemed to be rebuffing the effort. He decided to try one more time.

"Will you be at the theater tonight?" Stidham asked.

"No, I have to get back to DC. Something has come up. I know you have plans for Pickett, FIG, and Devens. I understand you will be staging in Guam. Is